LADY
SHERLOCK
· CIRCLE OF THE SMILING DEAD ·

LADY
SHERLOCK

· CIRCLE OF THE SMILING DEAD ·

BROOKS ARTHUR WACHTEL

Brooks Wachtel

To Kerry & Myra — The best neighbors in the world!!

WFP

WordFire Press
Colorado Springs, Colorado

ISBN: 978-1-61475-369-8

Art Director Kevin J. Anderson

Cover artwork image by Duong Covers

Book Design by RuneWright, LLC
www.RuneWright.com

Published by
WordFire Press, an imprint of
WordFire, Inc.
PO Box 1840
Monument CO 80132

Kevin J. Anderson & Rebecca Moesta, Publishers

WordFire Press Trade Paperback Edition November 2016
Printed in the USA
wordfirepress.com

ACKNOWLEDGEMENTS

I owe heartfelt thanks to many good friends for their help and support. Let me begin with Shari Goodhartz, my marvelous and insightful editor; Publisher Kevin J. Anderson and his staff at WordFire Press, for giving my book such a welcoming home; Peter Wacks, who had enough faith in an earlier draft to move this project forward; Tanya Lemani George and Donna Anderson, who inspired and were the visual models for Tasha and Deirdre respectively, as well as provided valuable feedback on the story's development.

In addition, I am humbly grateful to my brother Steve (who is so missed), Lena Pousette, Debra DeLiso (who is the voice of the upcoming audio book version), Barbara Alexander, Tom Bagen, Deepika Daggubati, the late Betsy Davis, Shann Dornheckler, Dan Doyle, Cynthia Harrison, Victoria Kirsanova (who modeled for the action illustrations), Tom Konkle, Mindi Miller (who brilliantly assumes Tasha's persona at conventions), Richard Mueller, Kathy Nolan, Nicole Nowak, Hilarie Ormsby, Brittney Powell, David Raiklen (who composed the wonderful Lady Sherlock theme music), Amanda Raymond, Leslee Scallon, Steven L. Sears, Donald Smiley, Terry Seabrooke, Shaene Siders, Sharon Spiro, Diana Zimmerman, Leslie S. Klinger (whose Sherlock Holmes course at UCLA Extension was illuminating), and Bernie Soon.

If my faulty memory has left anyone out—my apologies. Corrections will be made in future editions.

PROLOGUE

Heathrow Airport

Evening (1982)

Detective Inspector Julian Watkins marveled at the man's brass. The suspect was doing everything in his power to call attention to himself. Heathrow was one of the busiest and most cosmopolitan airports on earth, but even so, the sight of an elderly Scot, in full Highland dress, hobbling off the train, was raising eyebrows and drawing stares.

Julian, a tall man with a trim moustache, shrugged. While maintaining his distance, he followed the Scot up the escalator that led to the airline terminal.

The vast terminal wasn't too crowded, so Julian held back and watched as the Scot navigated through the building to an alcove containing several rows of coin-operated lockers. Julian kept as far away as he could; there was no way of following in there without being spotted, but then there was no real need for him to stalk any closer.

A discarded magazine, left on a chair, caught Julian's eyes for an instant. Perhaps one eye would have been more accurate, for he also kept the Old Scot in constant view. The magazine was an

American edition of *Newsweek*. The cover was an aerial shot of the aircraft carrier *H.M.S. Hermes*, and the caption, playing on a recent popular film title, read: "The Empire Strikes Back."

Hermes, along with the bulk of the Royal Navy, was on its way to re-take the Falkland Islands from Argentina. Britain was at war, and her sons would soon be fighting and dying. Julian had served in the Royal Navy, as had his father and grandfather.

The Old Scot passed two soldiers armed with automatic weapons. They had nothing to do with the burgeoning war in the South Atlantic; they were patrolling because of the I.R.A. and the interminable "troubles" in Ireland that had erupted once more, causing terrorists to plant bombs in England.

Julian was in the airport, not because of the Falklands or Ireland, but because of the Cold War and NATO. He smiled as he recalled the old curse about living in interesting times.

The Old Scot lifted the flap of the sporran in front of his kilt and withdrew a key. He gave a quick look around. There was only one other person nearby, a dumpy old woman about eighty in wrinkled tweed, wearing very thick spectacles and rummaging through her purse. The Old Scot ignored her, checked the number on his key, located his locker and inserted the key into the lock. Before he could turn it:

"Pardon me, ducky," said the old woman, waddling toward him with the gait of an ailing crab, holding a similar key and pointing to her glasses, "Can you read the number? My eyes …"

With a smile and a nod, he took her key and squinted at the number as she continued her lament. "Print the bloody things so tiny!"

He tapped the locker next to his and handed her back the key. She fidgeted, trying to insert the key into her locker. "Thanks, luv. It's rare these days to meet a gent what still knows 'is manners."

The Old Scot grunted in agreement as he turned his key. The two doors swung open simultaneously. He couldn't suppress a gasp, for to his horror, inside his locker was a colourful sampler with "The Jig is Up" delicately embroidered on it.

"Is something wrong, Mr. MacPhearson?" asked the Old Woman.

He spun to her as the sound of his spoken name caused the seeds of panic to sprout in his belly. She shook her head, reached into her locker and pulled out a large powder-blue envelope. The Old Scot gasped at the sight of it.

The Old Woman's eyes gleamed and her voice seemed clearly more refined. "Dear me, Mr. MacPhearson, dear me. I thought you had misplaced this. Very important, top secret NATO stuff, you know."

With surprising agility MacPhearson tore the envelope out of her hand and bolted down the row of lockers ... straight into two beefy constables who stepped out from either corner. He struggled with the strength of a much younger man, but it was no contest; he was rendered helpless in seconds.

Julian appeared and nodded, and the policeman extended the Old Scot's hands as the Inspector snapped a pair of cuffs on them.

The Old Woman, now smiling, toddled over, shaking her head in amusement. "It was the costume, Mr. MacPhearson. Such pretty young knees for such an 'auld Kiltie." With that she placed her hand on MacPhearson's face and ripped false skin away, revealing a man of no more than thirty. "Fuck off, Grandma!" was all he could manage and there was not a trace of the Highlands in his accent.

"Such language, Mr. MacPhearson! Or is it Mr. Grey? Or Comrade Kirsonova? Or Herr Von Kramm? Have I missed anyone?"

At Julian's signal, the police dragged "MacPhearson" away. Julian turned, beaming at the Old Woman, "Congratulations, Laura."

Laura settled herself comfortably into her old Bentley as it pulled away from the airport and, under the expert skill of her long-time chauffeur, entered the motorway for the forty-five-minute drive back to central London. Julian, in the jump seat, sitting across from her, pulled out a cigar and gave her a quizzical look. With easy familiarity, she nodded her consent for him to light up.

Julian settled back with a cloud of smoke swirling about him. "Fine bit of work. Really first-class. You've always had a flair for this foreign-agent business. Though, how you cracked this case by studying a half-eaten cucumber sandwich is what escapes me."

Laura wafted away some of the smoke with a wave of her hand. "You saw the sandwich."

"Yes. I saw it."

"But you didn't notice what you saw. Mother made certain I learned how to notice."

"Well, I think you're every bit as good as your mother was."

She leaned back in the seat and closed her eyes as the memories started to work their way through the years.

"My mother ... ah, she was something, all right. You know she wouldn't have touched this case. Hated espionage and working with the government. She preferred straight crime. Her first government case came quite by accident."

He nodded, "The 'German Flower Vendor of Nineteen-Fourteen'?"

Julian noticed a glimmer of sorrow cross Laura's face. "There was an earlier case. It even involved me. I was seven at the time. No one to this day has ever heard of it. Too many big people involved. And it nearly destroyed Mother ... she would rarely speak of it."

"Oh, come on. Tell. It can't hurt now!"

He beamed so much like an eager child begging for a story that Laura couldn't refuse. She sighed and smiled ruefully. "You'll sit and mope all the way back to town if I don't, won't you?"

He huffed in theatrically outraged dignity.

"All right. I was there for part of it. I'll tell you what I saw happen, what I was told happened, and what I deduced *must* have happened." Laura closed her eyes as she quietly remembered. "The world is so different now. Nineteen hundred and six might just as well have been another planet."

Outside the window was the familiar view of London. Towers of glass and steel dwarfed the Victorian survivors of a more elegant age. Laura cast her thoughts back, making herself see what was, and in her mind's eyes the huge towers faded away, the flashing signs vanished and the bright electric street lamps flickered into yellow gas. The speeding traffic slowed and the cars melted into carriages, horse-drawn drays and Hansom cabs. The noise of the modern city was gone, and she heard the clip-clop of hoofs against cobblestone. She started to speak …

CHAPTER ONE

London

1906

My singular and remarkable story starts a year or two after Father vanished. Mother was just establishing herself with the Yard and only Commissioner Rushworth Ramsgate really trusted her. Mother's first case was clearing herself of my father's murder (in fact, he had simply run off, unable to cope with her). Ramsgate was an unusual man. Tall, thin, and, save for the amused twinkle in his eye, every inch an old-school patrician with his elegant attire and aristocratic bearing. He came from an ancient and well-respected family and, had he cared about such things, would never have incurred their wrath by entering something as pedestrian as the police force. He was only a few years from retirement and thanks to a combination of hard-work, respect, and, it must be admitted, family connections, he was one of the most senior under-commissioners of Scotland Yard. Ramsgate reported directly to Commissioner Sir Edward Henry.

He was intrigued with Mother as he held a deep respect and, at times, I believe, awe for her abilities. He was just the sort of personality to be the lone champion of a woman playing a man's game, when all around him were scowls of disapproval. I also suspect that he, a long-time widower of around sixty, had a severe crush on my mother, the remarkable Lady Natasha Dorrington.

While some of Mother's cases were complicated, often the simpler ones afforded her the chance to practise her more colourful abilities, much to Ramsgate's delight. One he particularly mentioned to me involved her love of costume and dance.

Persepolis was, despite its palatial name, a modest eatery in London's immigrant-heavy East End. The entire area was razed by the Blitz in World War Two and it's a pity, for the owner of Persepolis, an émigré Persian, had personally done his best to make his place something out of the Arabian Nights. Belly dancing was scandalous, and it was that, far more than the ethnic fare, which kept the place busy. People from every strata of society enjoyed the veiled dancers, but on that night, a keen-eyed observer would have spotted one table where two men, intense in conversation at the very back of the dark room, were ignoring them.

The smaller man, clean-shaven and neatly dressed in working clothes, glanced around to make certain no one was paying attention. Then he produced a small velvet case from his pocket. The second man, heavy-set, with a goatee, placed a jeweller's glass to his eye, stroked his beard and examined the merchandise from inside the case—a diamond necklace. He replaced the glass in his pocket. Then, scowling, he took a water glass and used it to smash the "diamond" into fragments. The smaller man babbled in speechless amazement. Before either of them could act, a shadow crossed the table. They both looked up to see Mother, dressed as a belly-dancer, holding a small Webley revolver in one hand, while in the other twirling the real diamond necklace.

Ramsgate, sitting at a nearby table, walked over with a burly detective from the Yard. As the thief and fence were led away, Mother asked Ramsgate if he had any questions.

"Many—but let's start with, would you finish your dance?"

And she did.

Later that night, as the criminals were incarcerated, the thin one—as the constable roughly shoved him in the cell—cursed at Mother, calling her a "trollop." I recall Ramsgate mentioning that she stood in the dimly lit passageway between cells while most of the other prisoners, with good reason, glared at her. One large brute  growled, "I'll get you! There'll come a time! Mark my words! There'll come a time!" The other prisoners voiced hearty approval.

"Ah, the old song," she mused, "it's a ditty I hear so often of late." Mother was never known for false modesty. She waved a pert goodbye to the incarcerated assembly. As Ramsgate accompanied her out, she commented, "You may make the usual arrangements."

"Why won't you take credit, Tasha?" She allowed, in fact insisted upon, Ramsgate to use this familiar abbreviation of her first name. It was a decidedly unusual practice for that era.

"And have you stop bringing me all your little problems? I value the game, not the prize."

Mother walked a fine line between being useful to the Yard and not actively stealing their limelight. She was shrewd enough to know that the novelty of a woman detective would soon excite the press. The Fleet Street reporters only uncovered a few of her cases, but that was enough for them to christen Mother a lady Sherlock Holmes—soon shortened to "Lady Sherlock."

While Mother lived for the game, sometimes, when there was no intriguing criminal activity afoot, she found other—less positive—stimulations ...

The Inn of Illusion was one of the worst kept secrets in London. When Ramsgate stepped out of the Hansom Cab before the brightly lit mansion, the cabman gave him a knowing grin, which Ramsgate ignored. He walked—over a small drawbridge and a shallow decorative moat—grimly toward the door. He was certain of what was inside, for Mother, brilliant as she was, did have her frailties. I've suspected that she had a touch of what would later be called manic-depression.

Inside, the plump and severely dressed madam broke away from a group of scantily clad lovelies. She walked directly to Ramsgate and cagily asked if this was an "official" visit. He shook his head "no" and instantly the lovelies giggled and crowded around him. The madam asked in relief, "Which one?"

With the air of a man making the ultimate sacrifice, he simply said, "None."

As the amazed girls walked away indignantly, the madam understood. "Eliza?"

"How long has she been here?"

The madam led the way up the grand staircase. "Five days. She hasn't stopped. She's in the Cunard room, though Victoria

Station would be more appropriate to the way gentlemen come and go. Doesn't she ever tire?"

"Not that I've heard."

"Only heard. Pity. She's an odd one. *She* pays *me* and picks her own people. Never heard the like, but a quid's a quid no matter how it comes."

They approached a door with a ship's bell affixed to the wall near the doorframe. The madam hesitated, "She's with Captain Crocker."

"Seafaring man, eh?"

"It's all pretend—you know that."

They put their ears to the door and from inside they heard a deep voice yelling, "Stroke! Stroke! Stroke! By God Liza, you're bloody marvelous!" Then he started singing—off-key—"Blow, blow, blow the man down!"

Ramsgate reached for the bell, and with determined energy, clanged it several times. Inside, the man's voice yelled, "Blast! Sail clear, you scurvy bilge rat. Prepare to repel boarders!"

"This is Commissioner Rushworth Ramsgate, Scotland Yard!"

Ramsgate opened the door and stepped in. The room resembled a fanciful pirate ship. Plaster "cannons" pointed to the ceiling and the bed resembled a crow's-nest. "Captain Crocker"— a big man with a ruddy complexion, in his long underwear and sporting a captain's hat—gulped in genuine panic. Ramsgate offered him advice, "Abandon ship!"

"Every man for himself!" yelled Crocker as he grabbed his clothes, including a very land-lubbery top hat. He ran to the French window, threw it open, dashed to the balcony and leapt over the side. There was the sound of splashing water.

Ramsgate went to Tasha, who appeared a bit dissipated as she lay in bed, under the covers, but wearing a pirate hat and eye-patch. Save for her state of undress, Mother would have fit onstage at the Savoy's revival of *The Pirates of Penzance*. She smiled and placed a toy cutlass in her teeth. Ramsgate could only sigh; she was simply so charming. He gently removed the cutlass.

"Shall I take you home, Tasha?"

She quietly answered, "Yo ho ho."

These little escapes weren't Mother's only antidote to boredom.

The Penbrokes's elegant house, the crown jewel of the fashionable and exclusive Park Lane, radiated wealth.

Tasha, dressed in her tight, black cat-burglar outfit, silently opened the upper-floor bedroom window. There were few buildings that Mother couldn't scale. All she needed was the slimmest of handholds and, even under a new moon, she could scurry silently up the side of any domicile that was otherwise secure.

The two elderly Penbrokes were asleep in bed. Mr. Penbroke, his moustache hidden under a moustache-presser, clutched his teddy bear—an object, it was said, he'd be lost without.

Even if they'd been awake, Tasha, clad in black, would have blended into the shadows. She efficiently found the jewellry box and tossed a gigantic diamond into a little pouch. Just as she was about to make her escape back through the window, something caught her eye ...

Lady Penbroke's tiara, glittering in the faint moonlight, rested on the night table. Tasha reached toward it, but went past the diadem, and snatched the teddy bear. She deftly slipped it from Mr. Penbroke's embrace. As she left, Tasha thoughtfully closed the window so the crisp night air would not give them colds.

I used to love looking out our front window to the busy thoroughfare. I still do. I reside in the same house on Brook Street today, just between Hanover Square and Grosvenor Square (and not far from a house where George Frideric Handel once lived), though so much else has changed (the American Embassy is now nearby).

I would often try to emulate Mother's methods and deduce the occupations and lives of passing people. It was a great exercise in observation and imagination. Of course, I had no way of verifying my deductions, but with the certainty of youth I was confident in my accuracy. That day, as I hugged my new Teddy Bear and practised my vigil at the window, I saw Ramsgate striding furiously toward the house. I always adored Ramsgate; though not really related, he was like a loving and favourite uncle—unless he was angered. And irate he certainly was at that moment.

I bit my lip as he stormed to the door. Behind me, her head in a book, was Nanny Roberts. I mostly remember her head being hidden by a book. How that woman loved to read.

"He looks upset," I said. "Mother must have stolen something again."

The house nearly shook as the doorknocker slammed against the door.

"Something expensive," I added.

There was another very loud crash.

"Very expensive," I concluded gloomily.

Nanny Roberts lowered her book, and we exchanged knowing glances. "The Crown Jewels again?" I asked. Nanny raised her eyebrows. The possibility could not be dismissed.

Wickett, our butler, opened the door, but before he could even wish Ramsgate a good morning, the Commissioner entered and informed him that this was an "official call."

"Oh, dear. She is in the gymnasium, sir. I shall announce you."

"That won't be necessary," said Ramsgate as he strode toward the gymnasium.

"Oh, dear." What else could Wickett say?

As Ramsgate walked past, I popped up from behind a vase and as brightly as I could, "Good morning, Uncle Ramsgate."

"Good morning, Laura." He nodded and turned determinedly to carry on with his mission.

"Are you going to try to arrest Mother again?"

"I'm going to do more than try!" He continued his march.

"Will you still take me to Madame Tussauds Saturday?"

He stopped, sighed, and dully nodded as I walked away. "Laura, I've come to arrest your mother."

"Oh, you never do. If you did, who would solve your cases for you?"

He pointed to Teddy, "Where did you get that?"

"Mother gave Mr. Teddy to me this morning, Commissioner Ramsgate. He's my best friend."

Ramsgate drummed his fingers on the stair railing for a few seconds as he thought that over, then sighed and continued purposefully to the gymnasium.

Ramsgate boldly opened the door and marched in. "Tasha, my dear. Here's the warrant!" He produced the document from his pocket and waved it in triumph. "And here's the darbies!" He whipped out the handcuffs—then noticed that he was talking to an empty room. It was the largest room in the house, and in a more conventional establishment the prodigious area with its high ceilings might have even sufficed as a small ballroom. Mother had little use for soirées—but a keen interest in sweat. She replaced the crystal chandeliers with ropes and trapeze. He wandered in looking for Tasha among the amazingly rugged equipment. Along with dancer's barre, parallel bars, and rope, there were large weights, fencing foils, and a high-wire. Ramsgate leaned against the safety net bewildered, when he heard:

"You should not have left your office before the morning post."

He followed the direction of the voice and there was Tasha, suspended above him, effortlessly hanging from the rings, supporting herself with the strength of her arms in the grueling iron-cross position. She had designed her own exercise attire and it not only allowed complete freedom of movement, but was exceedingly revealing, displaying her shapely and well-muscled arms and legs.

"I haven't been at the office all morning," he said, trying not to show how impressed he was with her strength and overwhelmed by her figure. "I've been at …"

"… the Penbroke Estate," interrupted Mother, "vainly looking for clues regarding the disappearance of the Watusi Diamond."

"You are the absolute limit! It's not the diamond. It's the Teddy Bear!"

As I perched myself back at the window, I spotted a rough looking bruiser on the sidewalk observing our house. He was big, clad as a workingman, and in desperate need of a razor. He was scowling. "I think we have another caller—he's going 'round to the side."

Nanny didn't bother glancing up from her book. "He means ill for your Mother, doesn't he?" she said placidly.

I sighed and leaned on the windowsill and nodded. She just kept reading, commenting, "The poor innocent … elbows off the windowsill, dear."

I made a face and removed my elbows.

Mother, still on the rings, practised her gymnastics while continuing with Ramsgate. "You can't arrest me."

"Why not? Come down here."

"No evidence," she said as she twirled on the rings. I believe the distraction of her gyrations was why she failed to spot the brawler at the French doors of the gym. He cracked his impressive knuckles and gave an evil grin.

Ramsgate was still trying to pin down Mother. "But the diamond! The Teddy Bear!"

"I will not discuss the Teddy Bear. As for the diamond, I don't have it."

"Who does?"

Before Tasha could answer, the bruiser made his entrance by kicking open the doors and barging in. Ramsgate spun as the huge man strode in menacingly and pointed to Mother. "You Lady Tasha Dorrington?"

"I consider the question highly personal." And she continued on the rings.

The thug grabbed Ramsgate by the collar and made a fist. "Come down!" Ramsgate nodded in agreement. Tasha slid down a rope suspended from the ceiling into the net and then somersaulted herself to the ground with an aerialist's fluid grace. The thug let go of Ramsgate and stomped over to Tasha, who had started curling a large weight.

Pleased at anticipating this novel variation of her training, she announced, "Allow me to introduce Animal Rosencrantz, who could best be described as a 'for-hire' practitioner of physical persuasion."

"Charmed," said Ramsgate, dryly.

"Now employed by ... let me see ... Lord Carlfax."

Animal exhibited no surprise. Perhaps he simply wasn't bright enough to be surprised. "Right! 'e was none too chuffed about 'is wife discoverin' 'is addiction. Said to give you something." He grinned and loudly smashed his ham-hock-sized fist into his calloused palm.

Mother smiled and said, "Here," while tossing him the weight. He instinctively caught it and was thrown backward off his feet. Tasha continued to exercise and stretch while speaking to Ramsgate. "What were we discussing?"

Ramsgate couldn't keep his eyes off Mother. Seeing a figure like hers, taking exercise, was simply an opportunity almost unknown for a gentleman of 1906. "The Watusi Diamond." He replied at last. "You were about to tell me who has it."

As they talked, Animal regained his footing and attacked Tasha. She kept exercising and dodged every blow—all without breaking her conversation.

"You do."

"Me? The morning post!"

At this point, Mother went on the attack, using the movements of her exercise to trip and hit Animal, while otherwise ignoring him. "It was mailed to you. Disguised handwriting." A kick sent Animal hurtling into a heavy punching bag as Mother added, "Suburban post office—impossible to trace. So you really haven't much of a case."

The brutish Animal picked himself up and, in a rage, once more continued his futile offensive. He kept swinging; she kept dodging. He was nearly in tears.

"Stop movin'! You're like a bloody jack-rabbit!" he screamed.

"Oh, all right. Go ahead. Hit me." She stood still. Animal gawped at her dubiously.

"You won't stop me?"

"I promise," Mother said encouragingly.

Animal positively beamed.

Ramsgate watched in apprehension. Tasha stood nonchalantly while Animal, using all his body-weight, threw a fearful blow to her stomach. Tasha didn't even wince. Ramsgate's mouth dropped open while Animal massaged his stinging hand. Tasha shook her head sadly at him.

"That was pathetic," she admitted as she turned her back on Animal and walked to Ramsgate. "The criminal element of this city is not what it used to be—but then perhaps it never was."

"How ... how did you do that?"

Tasha answered Ramsgate, without so much as a glance at Animal—who barreled at her like a maddened bull. "Muscle control I developed when with the circus." She then back-kicked the charging Animal, sending him flying across the gym. She finished explaining, "The trapeze builds great strength, and belly dancing does wonders for the stomach."

Animal had fallen in a heap across the net. Ramsgate watched in growing amazement as Mother tossed the massive brute over her shoulder, carried him to the corner and dumped him on the floor. With little effort, she picked up a large weight—unlike a modern barbell, the weights at either end were permanently attached, sand-filled iron spheres—and placed it astride the unconscious man's chest. As his arms were pinned between the big iron balls and his body, there was no way he could extricate himself.

"I shall deal with this disappointingly incompetent opponent and his opium-addicted employer after my exercise."

Tasha started a challenging routine on the parallel bars, while musing, "When there are no criminals, no mysteries ... well, I use the police as opponents. It's the best I can do."

Ramsgate wandered closer—not entirely unsympathetic. "Someday, you'll crack one crib too many, slip up, and I won't be able to help you."

She did a handstand on the bars, bringing her face-to-face, upside down, with Ramsgate. She gave him her most disarming smile.

Despite the grin, Ramsgate thought she seemed very, very bored. He sighed in resignation. "Cheer up, Tasha. It's a big city. Something gruesome will happen soon."

"One can always hope."

CHAPTER TWO

St. James Park

A small, well-dressed boy appearing to be about five or six was searching the crowd. A brass band in resplendent uniforms (it was an era of uniforms) was giving a summer concert and making a lot of noise. The little boy scanned the people with an intense concentration exceedingly rare in a child, at last spotting what he was after.

A naval commander approached briskly toward him, through the throng—St. James Park was, even then, very popular. Clutched in the officer's hand was an official Royal Navy attaché case. Whitehall and the Admiralty bordered the park, and it was not uncommon for members of His Majesty's government to cut through the park, making their stroll more pleasant.

The commander was enjoying his walk and could see the scaffolding set up for the construction of the massive Admiralty Arch just bordering St. James. The officer smiled in satisfaction. Aston Webb's elegant design would contain two residences for the Sea Lords, but more importantly, greatly expanded office space that the new, twentieth century Royal Navy desperately needed, even with the addition of its newly completed Queen Anne-style extension now called "The Old Admiralty Building." The new First Sea Lord's reforms were shrinking the fleet while at the same time doubling the staff work. The palatial building, with its three distinctive arches, would be an impressive sight when completed. As if the monumental architecture weren't enough to remind everyone of the importance the navy played in Britannia's life, the Admiralty Arch would also form part of the ceremonial approach to Buckingham Palace. The commander noted with pride that Aston Webb had also designed the front of the royal residence.

The commander's attention was diverted as the little boy burst into tears and ran toward him. To an onlooker, it was just a child sobbing out some tale of woe to a man in uniform.

"I'm sorry you're lost, little man, but I'm not a constable," said the commander sympathetically. No doubt the child had mistaken his uniform for that of a policeman.

That produced more wailing and sobbing.

"All right," said the embarrassed commander. "Enough of that boo-hooing. I'll help you find your mates." The commander took the child by the hand, and they started to scour the park. Not far from the hard-working brass band, they came to a large curving hedge—it's still there, even today—and the child suddenly got excited, pulling at the officer's hand, yelling, "This way!"

The boy broke away and ran through a crack in the bushes. The officer shook his head and followed.

Inside was a small area, confined all around by tall hedges. The isolation might have been a warning, as was the sight that greeted the officer. The little boy had run to a slim Nanny, who was gently rocking a perambulator. There were three more little boys standing obediently in line, like the Nanny, their backs to the commander. The boy pointed to the officer and the Nanny turned around.

She was hauntingly beautiful, but in an almost mask-like kind of way, with large, aware, and intelligent dark eyes that held an intense gleam that was disturbingly sinister. She coolly appraised the officer—who stared in apprehension—and she said softly to her charges, "We must thank the gentleman."

The little boys turned around. One of them was smoking a cigar. They were midgets and, pulling out revolvers, they shot the commander. The noise of the gunshots had been covered by the overture to Gilbert and Sullivan's "Princess Ida" played by the brass band.

The "Nanny" snapped her fingers and ordered, in German, *"Abrufen der Kunststoffgehäuse!"* Which meant, "Fetch the attaché case." One of the midgets pulled it from the officer's hand. As he did, the woman asked sharply, *"Ist er noch am leben?"* The midget checked the officer's pulse and said, *"Ja."*

The woman snapped her fingers again and extended her hand. On one finger was an unusual ring: a blood-red pearl crescent-moon. The midget gave her the case, which she put in the pram. She wheeled it away as the "children" fell obediently in line. As the smoking "child" was about to toss his cigar, the woman shook her head. He crushed the cigar out in his palm and placed it in his pocket. They walked back through the hedge into the park, looking like nothing more sinister than a nanny and her charges.

Behind them, in the clearing, the badly wounded officer painfully opened his eyes.

CHAPTER THREE

Charing Cross Hospital

R amsgate and an over-cultivated fop of a naval officer (not that I knew what a fop was at that age), Commander Bernard, who seemed to permanently affect a supercilious sneer, huddled around the bed of the officer wounded in the park. The injured man was alive, but in great pain. They were in a private room. Charing Cross Hospital, located on the embankment, not far from St. James Park and Whitehall, was the most accessible hospital to the scene of the crime (and the most convenient to the offices of government). A senior surgeon, as befitted the gravity of the case, was having sharp words with Commander Bernard, telling him that he didn't want his patient questioned at this time.

Bernard, sniffing snuff, could have used a lesson in "bed-side" manner, for he simply dismissed the surgeon with a haughty, "I do so apologize, doctor, but you really must leave the room. Really must."

The doctor, not accustomed to being overruled in his own realm, walked to the door with a sneer. "I will allow you one minute before I send in a sister! And I insist you keep that snuff away from him!" With a parting glare, he closed the door behind him.

Commander Bernard shrugged. "Touchy, these medical fellows, eh?"

Ramsgate shrugged back, leaned over the patient. The wounded officer gasped with effort, "Ger ... Germans ... the Ger ..." then he sank back unable to continue.

"Fritz again, eh?" snorted Commander Bernard. "Bad show. Someday those Huns'll push us too far. Ask him for details."

Before Ramsgate could do that, there was a knock at the door, and the sister, a high-ranking nurse, announced herself. Ramsgate suggested the two of them come back later. Commander Bernard reluctantly agreed, and they left. The sister entered, closed the door and took out a hypodermic syringe from her apron. The glass cylinder clicked against her red pearl crescent-moon ring. She injected the injured officer, and he gagged, shuddered, and lapsed back in the bed as she mused, "You've played your part, time to exit the stage." She studied the dying man, her face a beautiful but expressionless mask. She bent down and gently kissed him. *"Auf Wiedersehen,"* she said.

CHAPTER FOUR

St. James Park

I don't like bringing in outsiders," huffed Commander Bernard to Ramsgate as they, and several constables, watched Mother examine the scene of the crime. She was on her knees, sweeping something on the grass into an envelope. She was dressed elegantly, but a keen eye would have noted that her outfit had subtle alterations that allowed freedom and movement, all while being fashionable.

As Bernard saw her withdraw a shiny, flat metal case from her reticule, he was further irritated. "A cigarette case! Is this creature going to smoke?"

Tasha threw him one of her practised superior smiles and snapped open the case, revealing her stylish Art Nouveau magnifying glass. Bernard coughed into his fist as Ramsgate, happy at not being on the receiving end of Tasha's wit for once, smirked.

Mother studied the ground. Then, oddly unexcited, asked, "Would you give me your interpretation of the events, Ramsgate?"

He was flattered she'd asked. "Delighted! I think it's obvious. Those tracks suggest some sort of wheeled device, possibly a vendor of hot chestnuts by the proximity of children's footprints." He pointed out the prints as Tasha nodded for him to continue. "The Admiralty courier came in here seeking a treat, the vendor, in reality a German agent, waited until the two of them were alone and then attacked the courier, though mistakenly failing to kill him."

"Why, Ramsgate. You really are coming along. You've observed every important clue."

He swelled in self-satisfaction. He should have seen what was coming.

Tasha concluded, "Incorrectly."

The swelling subsided. She continued. "The size and weight of the tracks, the location of the footprints and the length of the vendor's stride, indicate a singular exceedingly probable course of events."

The two men stared contritely at her. Mother was used to that. They motioned for her to continue.

"The conveyance was a perambulator pushed by a woman. Notice the narrow footprints and the dainty stride. The children—and the footprints indicate four of them—were midgets."

"How do you know they were midgets?" asked Ramsgate, with a hint of asperity that Mother ignored.

"There was no aimless wandering. Remarkably disciplined for children."

"But not impossible," insisted Ramsgate.

"Unlikely," Tasha said pleasantly. "Furthermore, children, as a rule, don't smoke cigars." She opened the envelope. Inside were ashes. "These ashes are always near a 'child's' footprints. He was a midget, and pretty well off, for this blend is a unique mixture from Bagen's of Edinburgh and costs sixpence an ounce."

"Never did like bringing in outsiders," grumbled Bernard.

"I won't burden you much longer, Commander. I shall call your consideration to two peculiar items and leave."

"Leave?" asked Ramsgate.

Mother ignored the question. "One. This area is isolated and away from the courier's normal route. The bait to lure an experienced man so astray must have been enticingly disarming. I suggest a midget disguised as a distraught child. Who could resist?"

"I, for one," offered Bernard.

"No doubt," agreed Tasha. "Two! The courier survived! That is very sloppy work, not at all in keeping with the calibre of planning we've seen thus far. His survival was deliberate."

Ramsgate raised his eyebrows. "Delib … why?"

Tasha smiled enigmatically (she practised that, too). "Ah, there you call upon me for a guess, and I never, in the absence of data, guess." She had read that explanation in *The Strand Magazine* and decided if she were going to steal, to steal from the best.

Bernard pushed himself forward. "Then just what, Lady Dorrington, are we to do with this information?"

"File it away. Here …" she pointed to her head, "… in easy reach for the moment when future facts will make it useful. Good luck, gentlemen." She started to leave.

"Where are you going?" asked Ramsgate as he hurried after her.

"Home."

"But the case?"

She stopped at the entrance of the hedge and shook her head. "I've given my advice. This is a government case. I wouldn't involve myself in that bureaucratic labyrinth for the world."

A few curious people had crowded near the entrance—the "nanny/nurse" among them. In fact, Mother briefly stood right next to her as she exited the hedge, followed, like puppies, by Ramsgate and Bernard. The woman overheard Tasha as she summed up.

"Just look for a woman and four midgets, although they're probably in Berlin by now."

"I hope not. Those missing documents are very important." Ramsgate could not keep the concern from his voice.

"What are they?"

Before Ramsgate could respond, Bernard cut him off. "That's restricted information."

Tasha sighed, her prognosis of government confirmed. Ramsgate knew when to back down. "All right. Look for a woman, eh?"

Bernard couldn't resist the chance to show off his wit, or what passed for it. "Now there's amusing work, so many to look over."

The woman, unnoticed, held Tasha firmly in her scrutiny. There was even a ghost of an expression of interest, especially when Mother concluded: "I can narrow the field for you. She's five foot eight inches, one hundred and thirty-five pounds, light brown hair, and has studied ballet. Good hunting."

The description fit the woman completely. The pity was that Mother didn't apply her knowledge as she walked past. The woman, in a knot of onlookers, averted her features as Tasha swept by, only to return her surveillance as the astute detective gracefully receded behind the crowd. Then, as if to increase her curious fascination, she heard Bernard telling Ramsgate, "That woman's deductions were all stuff and nonsense." But when Ramsgate answered, "Don't be so sure. Lady Dorrington is the cleverest woman in Europe." The woman's eyebrows arched and a smug smile flickered across her face. You could almost hear the unspoken, "Is she now … we'll see."

Ramsgate had one more salvo in my Mother's defence as he leaned in and said quietly, "And she can be trusted with secrets, Commander. Even ones concerning *Dreadnought*!"

CHAPTER FIVE

The Hermes Club

The Edwardian Age was an era of clubs, and most men of substance, and many not, belonged to them. The variety of these institutions was extraordinary, with clubs for gentlemen of every interest: military and naval clubs, conservative clubs, reform clubs, theatrical clubs, and even a club for the otherwise un-clubbable, where members were not permitted to speak to other members.

Ramsgate was a member of two clubs. The first was the Liberal Club, and he would often retreat to its sprawling, but solidly elegant abode near the embankment.

The second was the Hermes Club, a venerable establishment for people who belonged to other clubs but wanted to expand their social circles to include walks of life they might otherwise not meet. Within its elegant walls, an Admiral might share a brandy with a matinée idol, or a back-bencher from the Commons could defeat the Chief Justice in a rubber of whist.

That night, there was an element allowed that even this unconventional establishment usually excluded. The kind of persons not welcome in any club, no matter how conservative, liberal, or democratic. Persons shunned by these gentlemen's clubs because they could never be gentlemen—but they could be ladies. And four times a year, the Hermes Club allowed women—

these alien creatures—to cross its threshold.

Commander Bernard was also a member, and had, as I might have expected, misgivings about allowing women. He was losing a lot of money to one in a card game.

"Ladies' night should be once a decade, not four times a year!" Bernard complained, as he tossed his losing hand to the table and stalked away. His feminine opponent extended her fingers, reaching for his cards and revealing the crimson glow of her crescent-moon ring, contrasting with the forest green of the gaming table. She laughed and said, "Beginner's luck."

As she pulled over Bernard's losses, a tall naval officer in an immaculate dress uniform gave Bernard a mocking salute, and then grinned at the woman, noting her enormous pile of chips. The name of this strapping gentleman, I would later learn, was Commander Sebastian Blackshaw, and he was not there by happenstance.

Bernard ambled through the vast, restoration-era ballroom, past the various games of chance. The place had been converted into a casino for the night. Honouring the chairman of the entertainment committee's recent trip to California, many of the games reflected his romantic views of the American West.

The Chairman's efforts to revere his dime-novel (imported from America) understanding of the frontier was shared with another celebration, one which was a world away from cowboys and six-guns. Bernard had gravitated to a huge cake, in the image of a battleship, being sliced and served. Above it was an elegant banner that stretched across the corner of the prodigious room. "To our own Captain Summerlee—Commanding *H.M.S. Dreadnought*, Congratulations!"

Captain Summerlee was toasting his new command to the Assistant Chief of Naval Staff, both resplendent in dress uniforms that made them more dashing in appearance than reality.

"Congratulations, Summerlee. Navy's always been well represented here at Hermes, you know," said the Assistant Chief of Naval Staff.

"Thank you, sir. I'll try and hold the end up," said Captain Summerlee between mouthfuls of cake.

The navy was indeed well represented, for there were many uniformed men at the gaming table, and along with them, an almost equal number of elegantly-dressed women. None of the ladies appeared more enchanting than Mother, as she entered with Ramsgate. She was magnificent in a gown that showed off her figure to the limit of daring, though in this case Mother allowed it to be enhanced by a rarely worn corset. She inevitably shunned the constraints of that torturous device, and indeed, with her trim and athletic figure, really didn't require it. While she may not have had the artificially tiny wasp waist that a corset produced, her curves were sufficient to turn heads and stop conversation. Tonight, however, Mother surrendered to style and vanity, laced herself in canvas and whale bone, and gave truth to the adage that glamour was painful. They paused at the entrance. Towering above them was the famous statue of Hermes, the wing-footed messenger of the gods, and, more relevantly, the god of travellers and gamblers. Tasha scanned the room.

"Ah, the fleet's in! All those sailors," she teased Ramsgate.

"Rekindling youthful memories?" Ramsgate said a bit more rakishly than usual as Tasha threw him a tolerant raised eyebrow. "It's in honour of one of the members, Captain Summerlee."

"Yes, he's just been posted to command *Dreadnought*, at least according to the *Times* and *Daily Chronicle*—and they rarely agree on anything," observed Mother.

Less than an hour later, the gamblers at the roulette table gawked with admiration at Tasha's enviable pile of five-pound chips. Bernard, champagne in hand, closed in as Ramsgate commented to Tasha that the table was following her lead.

Bernard groaned, "Wish I had something left to bet."

"Run of poor luck, Commander?" said Tasha, with the barest hint of sympathy.

Bernard pointed to the card tables in the corner. "I was beached by that witch over there. Lost my entire allowance."

They couldn't see the "witch" through the crowd around her table. Tasha and the two men drifted over in time to see a portly vice admiral nervously studying his hand. He folded and withdrew from the game. Another player sat down, and the woman across from him rapidly shuffled the pack of cards. The dealer was the murderer of the Admiralty courier, no longer in the disguise of nanny or nurse, but in a spectacular deep green gown.

Commander Sebastian Blackshaw grinned at her expertise. Across from the commander and the murderess stood a very pretty young blonde in elegant, but proper and modest, attire—as if she wanted to draw no interest to herself—who watched Tasha keenly. Mother, scrutinizing the dealer, didn't spot that she herself was being observed by this fair-haired woman, who could not suppress a knowing smirk.

Ramsgate studied the game in confusion and asked Mother, "What are they playing?"

"It's a variation of poker, the American game that's *en vogue* at the French casinos."

Bernard huffed, disgruntled. "That woman has more luck than she deserves!"

"Luck has very little to do with it," smiled Tasha.

Mr. Heath was the Hermes Club's Acting President. He leaned forward watching as Tasha, with Ramsgate and Bernard behind her, shuffled a pack of cards on his desk. They were in his private office, which was shrouded in silence. Behind Heath, through the window, a little paddle steamer chugged by on the Thames.

The sound of the cards being shuffled in the otherwise hushed room focused everyone on Tasha. "Whoever she is, she's employing the Higgans' shuffle."

The men were bewildered. "I've never heard of it," said Mr. Heath.

"I don't doubt that, Mr. Heath," answered Tasha as she continued to shuffle. "I know of only five people capable of executing it."

"Only five!" said Ramsgate in disbelief.

"Three in the civilised world and two in the United States." Mother actually admired Americans, but she knew of Heath's affection for the United States and she loved to needle.

Heath sat back in his plush leather chair and was suddenly conscious of the formal portraits of past Hermes Club presidents staring down upon him from the walls. The severe faces—with their eyes peering into him—seemed to hold him in judgement. The club had never known scandal, and it was his duty to honour that pristine past and keep it that way. "Cheating! And in my term of office!" Heath shook his head and turned to the window. A fog was drifting in, obscuring the Thames.

Tasha riffled the pack and the sound turned Heath's attention back toward her. Now that Mother had his focus, she explained, "The Higgans' shuffle involves remembering the order discarded cards are replaced in the pack and dealing tops and bottoms in an advantageous sequence."

"That's impossible," laughed Ramsgate.

Mother dealt five cards and turned them over, one deuce and four aces. "That depends on the individual."

Heath stood up and, with his hands resting on his desk, leaned closer to the cards. The fog may have been thickening out the window, but the Acting President of the Hermes Club was starting to see light dispelling his personal blackness. He placed the cards in Mother's hand, "An individual who could be very valuable to the good name of the Hermes Club, at this moment."

Back at the table, the devious and cheating brunette was enjoying herself as opponent after opponent left the game poorer in pocket, but richer in their estimation of the female of the species. "Anyone feel brave?" she asked the crowd.

No one stirred to fill the empty seat. Then, at once, a large stack of chips was placed on the table and Mother gracefully lowered herself into the vacant chair. She smiled in a way that any woman could read as a challenge and murmured, "I thought you might be finding men too easy."

The woman's eyes gleamed at Tasha, and then she shuffled the cards. On her finger, a facet of her crimson pearl crescent-moon ring caught the light and flared. "Men are always easy," she replied in a whispered chuckle.

The pretty blonde and Sebastian exchanged furtive glances.

The woman added, dealing cards round the table while gazing at Tasha, "I do enjoy a contest when there is one."

"As do I. But I am usually disappointed," replied Mother with a slight bow of her head. Tasha examined her hand, said that she felt lucky and pushed over a third of her chips. The enthralled crowd buzzed, for these were heavy stakes. The third player, a fat gentleman with huge and unfashionable side-burns, gloomily scrutinized his hand and bet his remaining chips.

With a hint of humour, the woman in the deep-green gown asked for discards, but everyone played the cards she had dealt. The crowd around the table grew as people drifted over from other amusements. The dealer called; my Mother and the fat gentleman displayed their cards. The woman sympathetically cooed, "Poor little lambs." She placed her winning hand on the table.

The blonde and Sebastian shared satisfied smirk, but Bernard, Mr. Heath, and Ramsgate were worried. Ramsgate grew even more concerned when Mr. Heath whispered to him, "She's your guest. You're responsible for her losses, old boy."

Ramsgate nervously cleared his throat.

The game continued. Tasha pleasantly reviewed her cards, her face betraying nothing. The fat man put his cards on the table, admitting he was done. He wished the ladies good night and ponderously retreated.

"Anyone else?" asked the dealer as she settled back in her chair; her shining eyes taunting all around her. The crowd murmured, but no one moved to the empty seat. "That leaves us."

"It does indeed," replied Tasha venom-for-venom, and slid over a third more of her chips. The brunette matched the bet and they played. Soon Tasha, with a cocky nod, showed her hand and the mysterious woman did the same. Tasha's confidence faded. Once more, she had lost.

"Is this game too fast for the cleverest woman in Europe?" asked her opponent.

"I'm simply not used to playing for pennies." Tasha snapped her fingers and, as she had arranged, a tray with an immense pile of chips was brought to her. She slid the entire amount across. "Five thousand pounds are stakes that pique my interest."

"Oh, God!" Ramsgate gasped to himself, fighting down the panic. He had a savage vision of a suddenly threadbare retirement. This was, after all, an era when the average per annum salary of a professional man was 700 pounds.

"Are you good for it?" Mother asked casually.

There was absolute silence. The dealer, stung by the insult, almost imperceptibly—and only for an instant—clenched her fists. The blonde and Sebastian again exchanged clandestine eye contact.

Tasha continued conversationally. "After all, you're not a member. Some assurance would be required." Of course Mother wasn't a member either—no woman was—but she knew when to keep her mouth shut.

The dealer, now livid and not attempting to hide it, snapped her fingers and the cashier came over. "Will my previous winnings cover this?"

He gave a cursory consideration of her chips and, with the skill that had made him a local legend, replied, "No, ma'am. You would require an additional hundred pounds."

Tasha gestured sympathetically, giving a "what can one do?" shrug.

The dealer, now on the defensive, sat back, silently appraising the collected Lady Dorrington. She coolly removed her crescent-moon ring and placed it on the chips. "I'm good for it."

Sebastian stiffened slightly, but behind Tasha, the blonde's eyes widened in amazement.

"How nice," Mother replied.

The woman in green started to shuffle, but Tasha reached across the table and stopped her. "If you don't mind." There was a gasp as Tasha slipped the pack from the dealer's hand and began to shuffle. "I always like to deal on the third hand. A silly superstition I inherited from my uncle, the Earl of Higgans."

The woman's protest died on the word "Higgans." The game was up and both of them knew it. Her aware eyes focused on Tasha's hands, spotting the cards being dealt from the top and bottom. Mother's defeated opponent didn't even bother to pick up her hand, but smiled in understanding. Like two duelists, Tasha returned the smile. Across the table, the former dealer's spine stiffened. She snapped her fingers and in a bold voice ordered, "Champagne for Lady Dorrington."

Tasha gave a curt nod in appreciation. "Thank you, it was enjoyable."

Mother's adversary leaned in closer and regally removed the crescent-ring from the table. Her unblinking eyes remained fixed on Tasha as she defiantly replaced the lunar circlet on her finger. "We'll play again, soon, Lady Dorrington. I promise you a closer game."

The intensity of her gaze remained as this imposing figure backed away and stood. Her large eyes slid from Tasha to Sebastian, who only stared dully. But as if receiving an unspoken order, the tall commander stepped forward and offered his arm. The woman-in-green placed her delicate hand on his sleeve, but there was nothing subservient in the action. Although Sebastian towered over her, it was she who moved first and he who appeared to follow. Her proud bearing demanded respect and inspired fascination. The silent crowd parted as the couple made their way through the immense room without glancing back. As the last flash of her green gown vanished past the statue of Hermes, the tone of the room changed from stillness to riotous accolades as the crowd engulfed Tasha. Ramsgate fought his way to her. "You nearly gave me a heart attack."

"Who was she?"

Ramsgate shrugged. "I know nothing about her."

"Save for the fact that she manipulates and cheats at cards, has an iron-nerve, supple and artistic hands with indentations on the fingers suggesting she plays the harp, and a small stain on her index finger indicating knowledge of chemistry, neither do I."

At the door, the pretty blonde was also leaving, but first she turned back to glare at Tasha. Mother, occupied with the mob of well-wishers, didn't notice this unremarkable figure as she left.

The blonde descended the steps to enter an expensive Brougham carriage pulled by a pair of matching white horses. Inside, the woman humiliated by Tasha was still fuming.

"Are you good for it? She really deserves my best, this one."

The blonde sat next to the woman, taking her hand to gently stroke it. Sebastian gazed uneasily at the two of them and inadvertently compressed his fists.

"We've more important work. The *Dreadnought* sails in less than a week. If you involve this Lady Dorring—"

The brunette's imperious eyes flared, locking on him. He sat silently back in the seat. The blonde broke the silence. "Deirdre?"

The woman, Deirdre—I still shudder when I recall her name—replied without looking at the other women. "We are not in public, Coira. Address me properly."

"Priestess," corrected the chastised young woman. "Forget her."

Deirdre assessed Coira coolly and, with disinterest, withdrew her hand. In doing so, Deirdre's crescent-moon ring slid from her finger and fell to the carriage floor. Coira pouted and spun away as Sebastian retrieved the signet and extended it to Deirdre. She reached out, stopped, and then stared into the exquisite blood-coloured crescent-moon pearl, which shimmered in the light of a gas street lamp.

"Let's permit our brilliant Lady Dorrington to discover us," whispered Deirdre as she took the ring from Sebastian. "But not understand until too late. She couldn't survive such a failure."

Sebastian, worried, started to speak, but Deirdre closed those piercing eyes and leaned her head against the velvet cushions of the seat. "She does have a predilection for high stakes, doesn't she? We must prepare quickly. Do not speak for fifteen minutes."

As his Priestess lost herself in thought, Sebastian gave up any attempt at communication. He rapped on the carriage roof and they started off. The carriage pulled away from Hermes, vanishing into the thickening fog.

CHAPTER SIX

Lady Natasha Dorrington's Residence, Grosvenor Square

In the distance, the chimes of the Tower Clock could faintly be heard tolling 1:30 in the morning. Tasha, in a Hansom cab with Ramsgate, noted that her house was—as to be expected at this hour—darkened, save for a light burning in the sitting room—the room she used as an office. She peeked over at Ramsgate, fast asleep beside her, and nudged him. "Wake up. Open those eyes," she teased. He groggily responded. "I'm inviting you in," said Mother with a glimmer in her eye.

Ramsgate snapped wide awake.

"There is a client in the study."

His enthusiasm faltered and he exited the Hansom with a resigned sigh. "Of course. I might have known."

Tasha struck a match and surveyed the footprints leading to her front door. "Aha! Medium height, heavy build ... and if he's planted in my study at this hour of the morning, exceedingly desperate to see me."

She opened the door and they entered. Tasha took Ramsgate's overcoat and hat to a clothes tree already occupied by another overcoat dressed with a warm wool collar, a battered tweed hat, and walking stick. She carefully analysed them with both eye and hand.

"Discover any other interesting facts about him?" asked Ramsgate keenly.

"Only that he tends sheep in Scotland and arrived in London at ten at Euston Station."

"How do you know that? A speck of dust? A suggestive bit of mud?"

"The ticket is in his pocket."

"You really are insufferable."

"Let's not keep him waiting. He has grey hair, is unmarried, at one time had money but has it no longer, and owns a large dog. I suspect a collie."

In Tasha's study sat a dour looking, heavy-set man of about fifty. He tallied completely with Mother's observations. Observations which she took delight in sharing with him—a technique used to impress clients. He bolted from the stiff-backed wooden chair, his pipe nearly falling from his mouth, and in a thick Scot accent, "How did you ken aw' that about me? You must be a bana-bhuidseach!" He noted Ramsgate's confusion. "A witch!"

"It's a petty masculine conceit to attribute a woman's intelligence to the supernatural," answered Mother.

Tasha and Ramsgate sat across from the man—he gave his name as McGloury—in plush leather chairs in front of the fireplace. Mother arranged the seating so that she'd be backlit, making her difficult for McGloury to see while illuminating him for her. By McGloury's feet was a large, inexpensive, canvas travelling bag.

"I cannae think of a natural way you'd know so much about a stranger!" he protested.

Ramsgate couldn't suppress a grin. "You'll be sorry you asked."

Tasha leaned back in her chair with the air of ennui and sighed—as if the explanations weren't worth the effort. "Your coat contained traces of raw wool, hence sheep. Though you haven't been at it long, have you?"

McGloury bristled from his chair. "It's witchcraft!"

"It's your hands. City hands. Tender hands that have never sheared sheep or wielded an axe. A few seasons out in the elements and those hands will be your farmer's uniform. One can read so much from hands."

"Simple, isn't it?" shrugged Ramsgate.

McGloury, despite being a hard-headed Scot, considered his discomfort, "She cogitates a wee bit over fast for me ... But, go on."

Tasha obliged him. It was all part of her "you're in good hands" performance. "You wear a very expensive hat, indicating affluence. It is long out of fashion and in dire want of repair. Money, I may safely assume, is presently scarce. The shocking accumulation of dust on the hat decrees the bachelor. No good Scot wife would allow it. Have I omitted anything?"

"The dog?"

"Oh, yes. Teeth marks on your walking stick. Now, Mr. Cedric McGloury, as you fear for your life ..."

He grunted, "Aye. That's true enough. Something is trying to kill me."

Mother stopped him. "Something? Please be precise. Melodramatic inferences are of little help."

"D'ye believe in the power of demons?"

"No."

McGloury nodded, and then gave Tasha a hard grin. "Neither did I until three months ago. I inherited a wee croft. What you Sassenachs call a farm, from my older brother, Rupert. I've always wanted to settle down on a croft, raise sheep, so I moved in."

"Were sheep part of the inheritance?"

"I dinnae make myself clear, lass."

Mother's eyebrows arched at being called a lass—but she did not interrupt him.

"Rupert dinnae live on the croft," McGloury went on. "No one in my clan has for generations. Though we've held title for as far back as there were such things as titles."

"Why has no one lived there?"

"I dinnae ken, but we've tenanted the place as long as anyone remembers."

Tasha closed her eyes, mulling it over, and then asked. "Where is this demon-infested croft?"

"On Millport Island."

"In the Firth of Clyde, near Glasgow?"

McGloury nodded. Both men were impressed with Mother's grasp of geography. Tasha raised her hand before they could speak to ask McGloury, "The problem?"

McGloury took a breath, not sure how to put it, then simply stated, "I think I'm the victim of a curse. My sheep break out of the pen, no matter the precautions I take, and dash themselves over the cliff."

Tasha sank back in her chair, disappointed. Still, there must be more than this. Ramsgate gestured and gave a cursory laugh. "Well, that hardly sounds diabolical."

"You mentioned demons, Mr. McGloury," reminded Mother.

"Aye. Near my cottage are ruins, ancient cult ruins over a thousand years old, I'm told. The kind of place where the old ways still fester. Last night, in the middle of them, I saw a banshee."

Ramsgate smiled, but Tasha raised a warning eyebrow. To his surprise, she was taking this ghost story seriously. Ramsgate wasn't convinced and asked, "Isn't a banshee rather misplaced in Scotland?"

Tasha responded before McGloury could reply. "The western Scottish islands and Ireland share a common folklore in many instances. So you know the meaning of the banshee, Mr. McGloury?"

"Aye," he said seriously. "Death's herald."

Ramsgate, the very personification of practical and rational, blurted, "Oh, really! This is the limit, Tasha! The fellow's got a wizard imagination, but ..."

McGloury raised his hand to silence Ramsgate, and then reached into his canvas travelling bag. "Aye, Mr. Ramsgate, but tell me ..." He pulled out a large, cloth-covered object. "Did I imagine this?"

He dramatically whipped the cloth cover away, revealing the severed head of a goat. Ramsgate was repulsed, but Mother's eyes gleamed with excitement. She was delighted.

44

"That's wonderful!" She couldn't restrain herself. As McGloury bristled in protest, she motioned him back to his seat. "I mean, that's certainly interesting. A ritualistic sacrifice. Note the left to right incision. How often has this happened?"

McGloury regarded Mother in satisfaction, pleased that his problem intrigued her. "The sheep? Three nights at a time for the last two weeks."

"... but the dead goat and the banshee?"

"Only the night before last."

Tasha's mind raced. "When, to the best of your memory, did the last McGloury occupy this croft?"

McGloury scratched his head doubtfully. "That's a wee bit've history, now ... must've been back to Charles the First ... sixteen hundreds ..."

Tasha nodded and sat for several seconds, eyes closed, legs extended, fingers and palms together, oblivious to all. McGloury started to speak, but Ramsgate stopped him, pressing his finger to his lip as a warning. They waited in silence until Mother opened her eyes and walked to the window. Outside, the yellow orb of the streetlamp was just visible through the fog. Tasha stared at it, and mused, "If this danger is beyond nature, it is also beyond me." She turned back to McGloury. "However, I'll exhaust all other possibilities before admitting to hobgoblins. I'll accept your case, Mr. McGloury."

McGloury grinned, but it quickly faded. "I dinnae inherit much money. As you ... deduced, my means are modest."

"My fee is modest enough for your life," answered Tasha coolly.

"That's if you succeed."

"I never fail, Mr. McGloury," Mother said with passion. "I've gained acceptance in a masculine occupation because I succeed where all others fail. I am the final court of appeal!" She stopped abruptly, surprised at her own

outburst. Then she gave McGloury a pale smile. "If I fail, you won't be alive to pay me."

McGloury leaned back, not liking the sound of that.

CHAPTER SEVEN

Limehouse

McGloury alighted from a Hansom cab. He had left the warm fire of Tasha's sitting room less than an hour ago, but now, clutching his cloth travelling bag before a dingy, featureless building in the notorious Limehouse district, he was in a different world. As near as he could make out, through the pea soup fog, the entire area was dilapidated, derelict, and dying in squalor. A place of hard beginnings and sad endings, Limehouse was a magnet for immigrants, and had a sizable Chinese community.

McGloury walked to the door of the building and knocked three times, then three times more. A peep-hole slid open and briskly shut. The door opened a crack and McGloury slid through.

The place was long and narrow, with crude wooden berths, suggestive of steerage on an immigrant ship. He walked past the bent, cigar-smoking old woman who manned the door, then entered the smoky opium den. McGloury ignored the dreamers, puffing their pipes, some in strange positions, others mumbling incoherently in monotone, and went, purposely, to a tall, thin man sitting bowed over a small charcoal brazier.

The brazier had coins around its base. McGloury took one and walked to a door on the opposite side of the room. The walls of the place were stained and smudged brown from long exposure to opium smoke. He reached the door and placed the coin in a little slot. The door opened, and there, with a petulant expression, was Coira, the blonde from the Hermes Club.

McGloury entered a palatial room of polished mahogany and glittering crystal. The four midgets from the park murder were playing a game of whist at a gleaming wooden table.

At the far end was another door—this one of burnished, riveted steel.

Behind that door, the briefcase taken from the murdered naval officer in St. James Park had its contents spread across a table of glistening teak. Among them were technical diagrams of a battleship with "*H.M.S. Dreadnought*—Top, Top, Secret" in red ink atop the paper. A man in his late thirties, with a dueling scar, a thick neck shaved in the Prussian style, and a stiff military bearing, examined the diagram with his monocle. His name was Baron Wilhelm von Traeger, and he was dressed in a proper, almost severe, frock coat that he wore like a uniform. A Teutonic sense of bearing, as well as his heavy accent, betrayed his Prussian origins. "As we have agreed, Priestess, when the Englanders believe that the Germans have sunk their new battleship, they will certainly declare war."

Deirdre, sitting near Sebastian in front of a fire, was dressed in the white robes of an ancient pagan priestess. At first glance her robes might have been mistaken for Druidic, but there were differences that revealed the similarities were superficial; a scarlet belt accented her slim figure and a crescent-moon dangled near her breast, reflecting the dancing fire. She nodded and added, "Yes. Baron. That is why your firm and your English accomplices ..."

"Associates," he corrected.

She raised her eyebrow; the distinction wasn't worth a comment. "... have agreed to finance my plan. After all, war is good business when you make your bread and cheese selling steel and black powder."

"These days, cordite," he corrected Deirdre once more.

The room around them, the hideaway of the managing director of one of England's premier defence firms, seemed to give life to her statement. The decoration of the room was devoted to weapons: paintings and models of cannon, rammers crossed like swords, on the wall, as well as shells of various calibres. Above the fireplace was a huge painting of a sprawling armaments factory. Deirdre's chair was the cut-down bottom of an old-style 32-inch mortar.

Von Traeger tapped a chart of the Firth of Clyde with the edge of his monocle. A ship's course in red and marked "*Dreadnought*" skirted the coast of Millport Island. Another course, labeled "U-boat" originated from the island and intercepted the *Dreadnought* close by. "I will personally pilot the U-boat. We will be rich beyond imagination!"

"Money is of little importance, Baron."

He snorted, then with an amused smirk, asked her, "Then what you hope to achieve by this war escapes me, Priestess ..."

"I have my own accounts to settle. Some with considerable interest."

Von Traeger's voice became stern. "Then why do you wish to jeopardize everything with a personal vendetta against this Lady Dorrington? I will not permit it!"

Deirdre sat back in her chair and closed her large eyes, smiling faintly. Sebastian, concerned, inadvertently leaned forward. She said softly, "Do not betray me, Baron Von Traeger. Your own Herr Gottlieb attempted to interfere, and you remember what became of him?"

Von Traeger became subdued. "All they ever found was his monocle—polished."

"Am I in command, Baron?"

He clicked his heels and snapped to attention. "That was never in question!"

The door behind him opened and Coira entered, motioning toward the outer room. "He's returned from Lady Dorrington's." Her voice was sulky and there was an unpleasant slur on "Lady Dorrington."

Sebastian spoke up. "Oh, leave it be, Deirdre ..." but his determination dissolved as her eyes locked on him. He sat in silence and looked away.

Coira laughed insolently. Deirdre ran her gaze over the pouting girl in an almost masculine appraisal, then, bored, walked to the door. McGloury approached Deirdre the second he saw her, but did not speak until she asked, "Did Lady Dorrington ...?"

McGloury grinned and nodded "yes" to the uncompleted question. Deirdre smiled faintly and returned to her chair, commanding the attention of all in the room. "It begins," she whispered.

CHAPTER EIGHT

Lady Natasha Dorrington's Residence, Grosvenor Square

ickett carried Tasha's travelling bag to a waiting Hansom as she said her goodbyes to me near the front door. Behind sad little me, Nanny Roberts was just visible through the open study window, her head buried in her ever-present book.

I can still recall the scene with clarity. Whenever Mother departed on an adventure, I always tried to photograph her in my memory as if that image might be my last. She was dressed in travelling clothes of her own fabrication, which allowed freedom of movement, topped by a wide pancake-style hat with feathers. Her cloth bag, despite its small size, enclosed several changes of outfit. A parasol completed her elegant ensemble.

She kissed my forehead and reminded me to be a lady. I nodded. I wanted to tell her how worried I was with her venturing all the way to Scotland, and the little I'd heard about banshees and curses, but I didn't want to concern her with my apprehension. She knew anyway and was warmed by my silent concern.

I also remember that Mother's first love was her work. That she was unconventional was evident in her choice of professions. In an era when children were routinely raised by nannies and parents were distant figures of authority, Mother was often more distant than most, which made affection from her all the more treasured to me. My desire to win that affection first planted the seeds of my following in her vocation. I imagined the joy of sharing an adventure with Mother and strove to be as dispassionately attentive to details as she.

Mother gave me a hug and whispered into Mr. Teddy's ear, "Please tell your mistress that I'll be careful." Then she gave me a wink. "I promise."

I brightened up, and that won me another hug. Mother walked to the cab, turned back and called out, "Take care of Nanny!"

Nanny Roberts actually lowered her book and arched her eyebrows.

I dashed out to the cobblestones and watched pensively as the Hansom trotted down the street. I kept Mother in my view as long as I could, until the cab turned a corner and she vanished from my sight.

CHAPTER NINE

New Scotland Yard

Tasha stepped out of the Hansom, leaving her well-used travel bag on the seat, and told the driver, "Wait for me, Jarvey!" He nodded and pulled out a copy of the *London Times* (not a paper usually read by Hansom drivers). The headline proclaimed: "MURDEROUS ATTACK ON NAVAL OFFICER. *DREADNOUGHT* SECRETS INVOLVED." Tasha's eyes gleamed as she asked if she could borrow the paper. He handed it to her and she mounted the steps of the red-and-white brick gothic edifice designed by the noted architect Norman Shaw.

The building had been built in 1890 as the headquarters of the Metropolitan Police, but in this new century it already seemed slightly old-fashioned. There had been a vogue for Highland architecture at the time of its conception, so the building, whose bottom floor stonework had, fittingly, been performed by convicts, resembled a fanciful Scottish Baronial Castle. The force had already outgrown the building and an extension was being constructed next door.

As Tasha reached the entrance, Sherlock Holmes and Dr. Watson emerged. Holmes solicitously held open the door and Watson tipped his hat as Tasha walked past.

Ramsgate was at his desk while Commander Bernard was pacing. They both had cups of tea. Despite the crowded condition of the building, Ramsgate had a large, richly panelled office with a view of the Thames. A constable opened the door and Tasha walked in, hidden behind the outstretched and open newspaper. The headline was depressingly visible. From behind her journalistic wall, Tasha asked, "Seen the morning paper?"

"Hours ago," said Ramsgate as he pulled the paper away. "Behind the times, Tasha?"

Before she could make an appropriate reply, Sebastian appeared in the doorway behind her. "Sorry I'm tardy," he said stiffly as he nodded to Ramsgate, Bernard, and Tasha, who turned to him in surprise.

Ramsgate was in a fine mood. "Ah, the navy's here! Tasha, I don't believe you've met, Commander Blackshaw. Commander, Lady Dorrington."

"You had an interesting companion last night. Who was that singularly formidable lady in the green dress?" Mother extended her hand.

Sebastian kissed her offered hand. "I had never seen her before. And hope I never see her again." He let go of Mother's hand and gave a brief cough of embarrassment.

"Yet, she was your companion."

"Aye, but nothing more. I'm new to London. When Captain Summerlee invited me to the Hermes, well, I didn't want to attend alone. It was a friend-of-a-friend sort of arrangement."

Certainly Commander Blackshaw would have preferred to end the conversation, but Mother was persistent and asked for the lady's name.

"Her name is Violet Adler," dissembled Sebastian.

"Are you sure of that?"

"Well ... that's what she told me."

"And you knew nothing about her?"

"I was simply grateful not to go alone. You are very persistent with your questions."

"That is my business," grinned Mother.

"So I have heard. You caused quite a sensation. The evening was surprisingly entertaining. But I do apologize for my guest's behaviour, and may I compliment you on a superbly played game, Lady Dorrington?"

"You may call me Tasha. It usually saves people seventeen minutes a year."

"Eighteen minutes, seventeen seconds," came a rich, cultivated voice from the back of the big office. "You've miscalculated."

Tasha turned in the direction of the voice. A high-backed swivel chair pivoted toward her. Resting in it was the prodigious bulk of Mycroft Holmes, a man of Olympian detachment and vivid intelligence.

Ramsgate made introductions. "I believe everyone but Lady Dorrington and Commander Blackshaw knows the man responsible for our little rendezvous. Mr. Mycroft Holmes."

Tasha had heard of Mycroft and knew he held some post of dramatic importance in the government. Dr. Watson would later write that at times Mycroft *was* the British government. The only title Mother could discover him having was along the lines of "consultant." Whatever his official standing in Whitehall, his real authority extended high in the stratosphere of power and decision.

"I passed your younger brother as I was entering," offered Tasha.

Mycroft nodded as Ramsgate continued. "Commander Black-shaw has replaced the unfortunate officer attacked yesterday in St. James Park."

Mycroft elaborated. "The man was a special assistant to Admiral Fisher, the First Sea Lord."

Tasha was impressed. "Congratulations, Commander. I had no idea we were moving in such exalted circles."

Mother knew of Admiral Fisher, of course—everyone did. The amazingly energetic First Sea Lord, the nation's highest-ranking naval officer, had galvanized the navy out of a half-century of rigidity. By cultivating the press, and by his own forceful personality, he had aroused public and political interest in the Royal Navy to a degree unseen for a lifetime. His reforms included reorganizing the fleets, scrapping scores of obsolete ships and replacing them with smaller numbers of modern ships of new and daring designs. At the dawn of a new century, the tradition-bound Royal Navy had a leader with an eye on the future. And with the Imperial German Navy expanding night and day just across the North Sea, it needed one.

Ramsgate took a document from his desk and handed it to Tasha. "Exalted enough. What do you make of this?"

"It's on Barclay cream paper, written with a medium 'J' quill using Holton off-purple ink by an elderly man with asthma."

"Please. Just read it."

"Sorry." She read and was impressed. "Downing Street. It authorises my security clearance regarding the *Dreadnought*."

Ramsgate pulled closed the thick curtain and then lit the lamp on a magic lantern. The sleek image of a battleship was projected. Though the ship was barely completed, the silhouette—with its long snout and myriad big gun turrets—was already world-famous. Mycroft began to speak. "The *Dreadnought*, the ultimate battleship! With the firepower of any two ships afloat, she'll make Germany's entire naval programme obsolete."

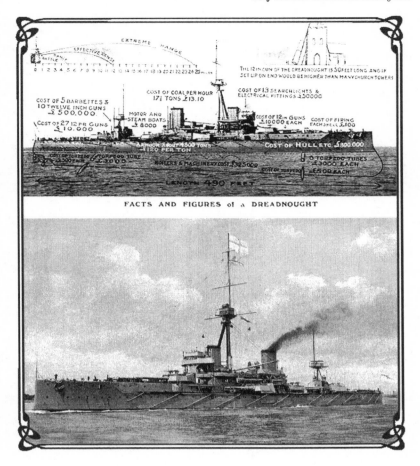

FACTS AND FIGURES of a DREADNOUGHT

"Why did they put the crows-nest behind the smoke-stack?" asked Tasha. "The smoke will blind the look-outs."

"We don't call them crows-nests in the navy," said Commander Bernard with asperity. "They are called fighting-tops, and it won't be a problem!"

The next slide appeared, showing diagrams of the *Dreadnought*. Ramsgate explained, "These are the stolen plans. Every effort was made to keep their loss a secret."

"And yet it was front-page news this morning," said Mycroft gravely.

"I can think of five theories to account for that, but the most likely is that you've been infiltrated," chided Tasha.

"Impossible!" stated Bernard.

Mycroft interceded before an argument could develop. "If anything would force this government to send an ultimatum to the Kaiser, it would be an incident involving this ship. She's become the very symbol of national pride."

"Or rather she was made that symbol through ceaseless government pronouncements," corrected Tasha blandly.

Mycroft raised his finger in agreement at her perception and then signaled for the next slide, which displayed a chart of Millport Island and vicinity.

It was Sebastian's turn to explain. "This is the Firth of Clyde. Up at the top is Greenock. That's where the ship is. Next week she sails on her trails to the Mediterranean and then the West Indies."

Ramsgate cut in. "Half of Whitehall's going up to watch her departure, and you can wager that the press will be out in force as well."

"The Admiralty will be very disappointed if they are not," said Mother knowingly.

"Look a few miles south of Greenock, Tasha," responded Ramsgate, sticking to his point.

"Aha! Millport Island. Where McGloury has his sheep farm. And since I'll be so close ..."

"I'm against it!" Bernard interrupted.

"So am I!" agreed Tasha, amazing him. "Gentlemen, I have a train to catch and a murder to prevent. Neither of them will wait."

Mother spun to make her departure, opened the door, and nearly collided with a messenger. Ramsgate, amused, took the message while teasing Tasha. "Pity. Seems we've ruined your exit." He read the note and his face darkened. "It's the medical report confirming, I regret, that our wounded officer has been murdered right under our noses."

Tasha took the note. "Murdered ... and all he told you was that he was attacked by the Germans. Why would they go out of their way to give us that information? Very odd."

"Then stay," offered Mycroft.

Tasha was polite. "I'm sorry, Mr. Holmes. The *Dreadnought* has 'all the king's horses' and such to look after it. All Mr. McGloury has is ..." she pointed to herself.

Mycroft nearly raised his voice. It was as much passion as he ever revealed. "Lady Dorrington! You have a misplaced sense of priority. The nations of the world are divided into two hostile camps and armed to the teeth. We hover on the brink of a war the likes of which man has never seen!"

Mother had no doubt as to the accuracy of Mycroft's statement, though his arguments failed to sway her. The case already involved Whitehall, Naval Intelligence, and Scotland Yard. No doubt the Intelligence Division of the Foreign Office and Diplomatic Service would soon be agitating to put their oar in (the Secret Service Bureau—a genuine intelligence service— would not be formed for another three years). Her freedom of action would be constrained, her methods questioned, her deductions doubted. She wanted no part of it, especially with the formidable and bizarre McGloury business before her.

"Your battleship will have to fend for itself. Good day, gentlemen," said Mother firmly. "I have never failed anyone who has come to me for protection. My client is my priority." She left, closing the door behind her. The men glanced at each other in bewilderment.

"Women!" mused Mycroft. "Can one trust even the best of them?"

"Especially that one!" answered Bernard whole-heartedly. "Who does she think she is? She struts around like a one-woman assault on the natural order of male supremacy."

Sebastian shut off the magic lantern and opened the drapes. Down on the street below, he saw Tasha enter her Hansom and drive off. He felt a sudden surge of apprehension.

CHAPTER TEN

The *Royal Scot* & the Ferry to Millport Island

 mail sack was unhooked from its pole and flung into the postal car of the *Royal Scot* as it rattled, at fifty miles an hour, toward Glasgow. McGloury had been late to meet Mother at Euston Station.

He dashed through the great hall, his single travel bag gripped tightly in one hand while vigourously waving his walking stick in the other. He reached the platform and, tossing his bag ahead of him, jumped into the compartment as the train was starting to move, precisely at ten (the London and North Western Railway waited for no man who did not have a weighty title). The train pulled away. McGloury, quite out of breath, nodded to Mother. Out the window, before too much time had passed, the city of London gave way to the greener home counties.

McGloury, new to farming, had been explaining to Mother, in excruciating detail, the tribulations of crofting, raising sheep, weather, and his recently acquired expertise on the uses of fertilizer. Normally Mother was keen on acquiring knowledge on a plethora of subjects. She maintained that you never knew when mastery of an odd fact might come in use. But after three quarters of an hour, she felt that the subject had been more than exhausted. Tasha was about to reveal that her interest in manure was limited, when McGloury noted the scenery that flashed by out the compartment window. "That's a bonny bit of country out there."

Speeding by were neatly laid out farms, with orderly stone walls set amid a landscape of fertile green. It appeared so safe and serene.

"'Tis a wee garden compared to Scotland," continued McGloury, as he rhapsodized about his native land. "And green, you dinnae know green 'til you stand on the banks of Loch

Lomand with the highlands beckoning in the mist." Then he gave a sigh and admitted, "But I must admit that, aye, these English farms have a simple charm."

"They do indeed, Mr. McGloury."

He gave a short laugh. "Now, you're not saying that a fine lady like yourself would bide awhile tramping the fields or clambering over cattle fences?"

"It might surprise you to know that I spent a summer's week on a farm just two stops up this very line."

"Were you on holiday, then? Pretending to be a country mouse?" he asked with a laugh.

Mother sighed with pleasure as the memory came back to her. "It was invigorating. The corpse of the owner's father-in-law was strewn about six different points of the stable. Just finding all the pieces presented a challenge. Still, I was able to clear the poor farmer. Though I am certain there are nights when he wishes his wife was at his side, rather than in Pentonville prison, despite her facility with an axe."

McGloury gaped at Mother for a moment, and then asked her to hand him the newspaper sitting on the edge of the seat. He made a point of being immersed in an article, his desire for conversation suddenly satiated.

"I think I'll indulge in a nap," said Tasha. "You don't mind, I trust?"

"Not a wee bit!" he replied.

Mother closed her eyes. They had a long trip ahead.

Although Glasgow was a modern city, and the Clydebank was one of the great ship building centres of the world, the only transportation to Millport Island was a single little ferry, scarcely more than a lifeboat with a steam engine, that left from the mainland town of Largs. Eventually, it would retire to the Glasgow Transport Museum, but in 1906 it still plied endlessly between Millport Island and the mainland.

The boat lurched in a heavy swell and spray inundated Tasha and McGloury, the only two passengers (save for a cow mooing in discomfort toward the bow). The ferry captain, a type referred to at the time as a "grizzled old salt" or when being affectionate, "Jolly Jack Tar," took a tarp from a chest in the stern, strode past his human fares and covered the cow.

Tasha raised her voice, overcoming the engine and the water. "Is this the only transportation to the island?"

McGloury nodded stoically, and they both huddled from the spray.

Tasha contemplated the dark water below with satisfaction. She loved swimming, and not just because of the exercise, but for the way that water—even when near frigid—engulfed her and simultaneously buoyed her up. She shifted her attention toward the bow of the boat.

Ahead was Millport Island, with its little town and crofts scarcely touched by modernity. Earlier that day she had seen, as if in contrast, the towering hull of the new Cunard liner, *Lusitania*, at the John Brown & Company shipyard on the Clydebank. The ship was almost ready for launching. She would be the most modern and fastest ocean liner yet built. It was indicative of the turbulent era that the government had helped finance the *Lusitania*, and her sister ship the *Mauretania*, on the condition that in time of war, they could be used as auxiliary cruisers. Even in peacetime, the public would get something for the expenditure of money, for these swift ships were expected to keep the Blue Riband, the accolade for the fastest Atlantic crossing, firmly a British possession (there would be no physical trophy until 1935). Tasha mused that while she would spend the night only a few miles from this triumph of advanced technology, her abode would have no electricity, gas, or plumbing.

CHAPTER ELEVEN

The McGloury Croft

Tasha and McGloury rode a gig, a one horse, two-wheeled cart, up a slight incline on a very bumpy dirt road. McGloury halted the horse and pointed below them. "There it is, lass. My bonny wee croft."

To a Scot, almost everything was "wee." I once heard a Scot call the gigantic ocean liner *Queen Mary* a "wee boat." However, McGloury was being more accurate than colourful. There was a thatched roof cottage near a sheep pen clustered close to a cliff with a mean drop to the water below.

By day, the place was more picturesque than sinister, but there was something else. About fifty yards from the cottage, adding a bizarre touch, were a group of ancient pagan ruins.

They were tall, rectangular dolmens, arranged in a semi-circle around an altar, crudely carved with agonized and brutal human faces, an eerie blend of Stonehenge and Easter Island.

Tasha was pleased at this eldritch stage upon which she found herself a major player. "Lovely, Mr. McGloury. A worthy setting."

In front of the croft, near the sheep pen, a thickset man with stiff bearing sat astride a horse. The rider was arguing with a young man in working clothes and a long wool vest, who gestured wildly. Standing beside the horse and its expensively attired rider, were two burly field hands. On a signal from the mounted man, one grabbed the young man and moved him away from the sheep pen's gate. The other of the big men held a sheep on a rope leash.

McGloury scowled, "There's trouble! That's Laird MacGregor! And they're accosting my ghillie Tom!" Tasha knew that a ghillie was Scots for a croft's hired hand, and that Laird MacGregor would be called Lord MacGregor south of Hadrian's Wall.

She held on as McGloury flicked the reins, sending the cart gamboling toward the croft. He pulled to an abrupt stop, jumped out, and ran toward the Laird. Tasha stayed behind in the cart, observing.

The Laird pointed his riding crop at McGloury, "You've been caught clear and fair, McGloury! Alec! Show him! Sean, let the lad loose!"

As the Laird turned his face, Mother got a good look at him. Tasha was not an easy mortal to surprise, but this revelation caught her genuinely unawares. It was none other than "Captain Crocker" from the Inn of Illusions. The same man who had leapt out the window of the Cunard Room when interrupted by Ramsgate. The Laird—and Mother would have to cease thinking of him as the imaginary "Captain Crocker"—hadn't spotted Tasha, as he was signaling his men. Sean let Tom loose and Alec brought forward the sheep. Tom, the ghillie, rushed to McGloury.

"He wants to look o'wer the flock. I dinnae let him."

"Good lad," said McGloury, still glaring at the Laird.

The Laird merely cocked his head toward the sheep, "Look at your mark, McGloury—go on, man. Use your eyes!"

McGloury inspected the dye mark, the "brand" on the sheep. It was blue, but tinted red unevenly around the edges.

"Do you see the red, now?" demanded the Laird.

"Aye! There's nothing wrong with my vision!"

"And do you recall that my mark is red?"

Tasha just watched, enjoying the confrontation. McGloury shoved the sheep away and spun to the Laird, towering above him on his horse. "Listen to me, Laird MacGregor. You may own the best land on Millport, but you dinnae own this croft, you dinnae own me sheep and you dinnae own me! So a good day to you!"

"You deny that this sheep is mine?"

"Man, I deny nothing! But it's travelling overfast to accuse me of thievery!"

"Half the flock in that pen have, or had, my mark! Alec! Sean!" At his signal they moved toward the sheep pen. McGloury and Tom tried to block them but the struggle was brief as the bigger men tossed them aside. While they did that, Tasha walked to the pen's gate, leaned against it and folded her arms, strategically lowering her head so that her wide hat hid her face. Alec and Sean approached her, but not wanting to assault a lady, gestured to their Laird for guidance.

Laird MacGregor, not recognizing Mother with her face hidden, tried to be civil. He asked her to step away from the gate. With her pugnacious visage masked by her hat, she shook her head. MacGregor altered from polite to persuasive, as he barked to the larger of the two men. "Alec, move her! Be gentle … if you can!"

Alec nodded and grasped Tasha's arm. She spun and smashed him into the fence. He stumbled to his feet in amazement. "I slipped! You aw' saw that!"

"Of course you did," offered Mother as she grabbed him and flipped him into the sheep pen. Sean, the smaller of the Laird's men, moved forward carefully. Tasha crossed her arms and grinned challengingly at him. He came close and, with hesitation, stretched out his arms to lunge at her. Mother directly eyed MacGregor, smiled and said, "Captain Crocker, I presume."

Laird MacGregor could barely get out the word "Stop!" rapidly enough.

Sean, arms still poised to grapple, stood fast as MacGregor reached into his coat pocket and withdrew a pair of glasses, bent closer and stared at Tasha. "Eliz—" He cut himself short.

Mother cocked her head. "Stroke."

MacGregor wheeled his horse around and shouted to his men. "Come away, lads. There's work to attend to."

Tasha leaned back against the fence as Alec climbed out of the sheep pen and strode wrathfully over to her. "You havenae heard the end of this."

MacGregor cut him short, ordering him back to the manor. Alec gave Mother a final glare and stalked to the Laird. MacGregor cocked his head to get going, and his two men headed down the road.

MacGregor paused and leaned closer to Tasha. "You don't think you could have mistaken me for someone else?

"A mistake is always possible."

"Very possible." He responded with a threat in his voice as he moved toward the road, passing McGloury. "I can't stop you living here, but stay away from my flock."

Tasha walked closer, "If you have a problem, there's always the police."

MacGregor laughed at that and galloped off, soon over-taking his men.

McGloury, with an air of satisfaction, shouted to Mother's enjoyment, "And dinnae come back! Tom, fetch the lady's things."

Tom got Mother's bag from the cart and hefted it to the cottage. Tasha inspected the surroundings one more time. "I take it Laird MacGregor wants your croft and you declined to sell it."

"Aye."

"It's curious that you are losing sheep and he thinks you are stealing his."

"There's not much grazing, flocks get mixed ... but you and Laird MacGregor seem to know each other."

Tasha merely shrugged. "We might have crossed paths on holiday."

McGloury snorted. "Aye. With a wife like his, I've no doubt he needed one." He held open the door as they entered the cottage.

That night, against the sunset, the tall crumbling stones seemed even more abnormal. Tasha ran her finger over the craggy lips of one of the granite faces. Something caught her eye. There was a crescent-moon carved into one of the monoliths.

"We've met before ... somewhere ..." mused Tasha.

All around her, a thick fog started to roll in from the firth. Within the hour, one could barely make out the feeble light of the cottage from the ruins.

The cottage was a sparse, two-room affair with a stone fireplace, big iron swing kettle and up-to-date furniture. It was quite comfortable. They had finished their supper of penny potatoes and haggis. Tasha and McGloury sat—at Tasha's insistence—in the most uncomfortable chairs McGloury owned. Her strategy was only partially successful, for although Mother was awake and alert, McGloury was snoozing.

Then Boab, McGloury's collie (of the teeth-marks-on-the-walking-stick fame) stirred, aware of something, and started to whine. Tasha turned down the lamp as Boab barked more intently and clawed at the door.

Outside, something was agitating the sheep. They shifted back and forth in the pen, pushing against the wooden fence.

Tasha, her eyes gleaming, and McGloury, awakened by Boab's barking, both rushed to the window. They saw that somehow the sheep pen gate was open—but the flock wasn't stampeding. A few sheep near the gate wandered out, but most of the flock stayed in the pen.

McGloury, fearing for his livelihood, raced out the door, with Tasha directly following. Tasha ordered him back to the cottage, but he refused and dashed to the pen, slamming the gate shut, while Mother chased the few of the flock that had escaped. She had valuable assistance from Boab. The collie knew his business and ran and barked, herding the sheep.

"Look out for the cliff!" shouted McGloury as Mother ran in that direction. The warning would have been better intended for the sheep, for a few of them tumbled over the cliff to the invisible sea below. Tasha lunged for one lamb about to fall over the edge. She pulled it by the leg and dragged it to safety, then carried the bleating animal back to the pen. With Boab now quietly at his side, McGloury accounted for his sheep. Tasha let the lamb into the pen as McGloury closed the gate.

The night was suddenly deathly quiet. Tasha studied the ruins—no more than a dark vagueness in the fog.

"I cannot protect you if you disobey me!" said Mother sternly. McGloury gave her a contrite nod, and Tasha, McGloury, and Boab walked back toward the cottage when a new sound drifted across through the fog: a mournful wailing, feminine, eerie, and sad, coming from the ruins. Standing amid the stones, and hardly distinguishable in the mist, was the lone figure of a shrouded woman, seen and vanishing at the whim of the fog. The spectre's skull-like face was barely visible, and her haunting wail beckoned.

Tasha was not easily convinced of apparitions. "That's a lot of wind for a ghost." She moved toward the ruins, but McGloury, terrified, grasped her arm. Tasha broke free. At that moment, the wailing ceased and there was only silence.

The ruins were empty.

Tasha scowled at McGloury for interfering with her, but as he was so shaken, she softened and said quietly, "You'd better go inside."

He nodded, and they walked to the door, but Boab barked at something toward the ruins. Tasha stared into the mist and listened intently. An indistinct figure ran from the tall dolmens. Boab barked and growled. McGloury, sensing danger, grabbed the dog's collar to hold him.

The figure suddenly screamed a woman's scream and staggered. Tasha heard a muffled, hoarse cry that seemed to say "Deirdre!" Then the figure screamed in pain, lurched to the cliff and, shrieking, flung herself over the edge.

Boab broke free of McGloury and dashed into the fog. Tasha cautiously moved to the cliff and gazed over the edge, noting how it disappeared into the mist below. The crashing of the surf was markedly audible. McGloury came up behind her. "Who is Deirdre?" asked Tasha.

"I dinnae ken."

Mother nodded and they walked back toward the light of the cottage. McGloury called for Boab, but was answered only with silence. He called again. "Now where is that dog?" They both searched the fog for him. "It's not like him to not come," worried McGloury.

Tasha's eyes fell upon the ruins, grim and silent in the swirling mist. She realised how exposed they were out in the open. "Look for him in the morning," she advised.

Her sense of danger was communicated and McGloury did not argue.

As they walked back to the cottage, they were being watched from a tiny hole atop one of the dolmens, high above unaided reach. The hole, through a series of tiny tunnels and mirrors, sent a shaft of light deep underground.

CHAPTER TWELVE

The Caverns, Deirdre's Chamber

The image of McGloury's cottage, with Tasha and McGloury entering, was projected on a round, polished stone by a *camera obscura*. The device, carved at the arched top of the chamber, was another hideous face, but this one was different than the tortured faces on the dolmens above. Hewn from the granite was a horned demon with a mouth of sharpened teeth distorted into an exaggerated death-smile. One of its eyes was a glittering red crystal, while the other eye projected the image in a beam of white light. The ragged ceiling that arched to this massive central face was filled with other carved visages. These did resemble the tormented sculptures with their silent screams from above, but they were turned away from the demon face as if too terrified to contemplate it. Though this terrible place no longer haunts me, it is still vividly engraved upon my mind.

The chamber was small and dimly lit by oil lamps, and the furnishings were simple save for an ornate four-poster bed and an elaborate harp. Deirdre, her face mask-like and inscrutable, watched as on the polished stone was projected the image of Tasha and McGloury entering the cottage and closing the door. Deirdre was still dressed in the banshee "shrouds" that Tasha had seen indistinctly in the ruins. The priestess pulled a lever, the light was blocked from above, and the image went dark.

"Lady Dorrington will be a brilliant opponent; you'll be earning every quid." She was speaking to a man, sitting in the shadows cleaning a large revolver. A table was covered with charts, maps, a decanter, crystal glasses, and a mortar and pestle. "Are you prepared?" she asked.

The silhouette answered by snapping the revolver shut.

"Then enjoy," said Deirdre brightly.

CHAPTER THIRTEEN

The McGloury Croft

Tasha, dressed for the outdoors, but allowing herself the greater protection that a larger pancake hat provided from the sun than her usual fore-and-aft, was at the cliff, examining the ground with her Art Nouveau lens. McGloury, a bowl of porridge in hand (do the Scots ever eat anything else for breakfast?), was between her and the ruins, calling for Boab. The flock bleated noisily in the pen. Behind them, the dark water was speckled with white caps and topped by a grey sky.

Tasha, finding footprints and broken shrubs, located the spot where the girl had gone over the edge. Below, water crashed against jagged rocks. With the tides and currents, Mother knew better than to waste time looking for a body in that black water. McGloury, in mounting frustration and growing concern, continued to call for his collie.

Tasha ignored him and inspected the footprints, which revealed the victim wore modern shoes that were irrefutably a woman's. Then a tiny dart, half-hidden under a shrub, caught her eye. She carefully picked it up, sniffed it, smelled something, which alerted her suspicions, and wrapped it in her scarf.

Just then a young man's voice shouted McGloury's name from the road. Tasha looked up to see Tom waving excitedly as he pedaled his bicycle off the road toward them.

Before he could speak, McGloury stalked angrily toward him. "Oh, at last! I know one tardy ghillie that's about to find himself seeking employment at another croft!"

"Aye, it's late I am, but there's a big to-do in the village." He started to explain as Tasha listened with interest.

CHAPTER FOURTEEN

Millport Village, The Spotted Dog

The body was laid across the bar and draped with a sheet. Tasha uncovered the face. It was Coira, the blonde from the Hermes. She was almost a caricature now, with her face twisted into a hideous grin, her eyes unnaturally wide open. Mother did not recognise her. In all fairness, she was rather pre-occupied the one time she saw this woman, and the blonde was simply another face in a large crowd. Mother liked to give the impression that absolutely nothing escaped her notice, for she did see far more than most, but she wasn't infallible. "Who was she, Inspector?"

She was speaking to Inspector Ian Taggert. He was in his mid-thirties, ruggedly handsome, dressed for the outdoors (with American-style cowboy boots), standing behind her and referring to his official notebook. Also present was bulky Constable Blake, the local officer.

They were in the Spotted Dog, Millport Village's sole pub, a long, simple establishment. Unadorned wooden tables and chairs took up most of the room. A short bar was at one end and a stone fireplace was across from it. The place was empty (not surprising as it was prohibited hours), except for the potman, who was closing the shutters, ending the show for the crowd at the window.

Ian answered her. His accent was not western Scotland, but Western America. "No one 'round here knows her. A fisherman found her in the firth. The local sawbones said death by drowning." He flipped shut the notebook.

Tasha liked Americans. She was a great admirer of America despite the occasional flippant remark she might make. Mark Twain was among her favourite authors. "An American. How charming," she said, noting his hands. "And one that rides horses and tosses a lariat. A cowboy! Aren't you a little far from your watering hole, Inspector …" Her voice trailed off, giving him an opening.

"Taggert. Ian Taggert. An' I reckon you can call me Ian, ma'am. There's no getting 'round that I was reared in Montana, but I was born here on this island. My folks emigrated to the States when I was a young 'un."

"And you couldn't resist the tug of the old sod. Delightful. Now, when you get this young woman's autopsy report …"

"I don't reckon there's a need for an autopsy, ma'am." He was being polite.

"What compelling curiosity." Mother was not being polite. She sensed resistance and was determined to cut through it rapidly. She flashed her most endearing smile and moved some hair away from the girl's neck revealing a tiny, discoloured, puncture wound. Tasha noted, with satisfaction, Ian's amazement. "I 'reckon' you realise that those facial contortions did not result from drowning and that the state of rigor mortis is too advanced for the cold water of the firth. Eh, 'partner'?" She jabbed the girl with her finger—the skin was like wood.

Ian strained to keep himself under control. "Don't let the drawl flim-flam you. I know my job."

"How reassuring," said Mother engagingly, "I needn't add, in that case, that she has been poisoned by some powerful vegetable alkaloid administered by…. well, why go on? You tell me."

He stared at her, near eruption. Mother, ignoring his mood, held up the dart to his face. "By this!" she said in quiet triumph.

Ian took a deep breath. "I'll just take that, ma'am."

She withdrew her hand. She'd made her point, now was the time to make peace. "Look, 'sheriff' …" She couldn't resist that one. "Why don't we arrange a little 'horse-trade'? Your full co-operation for mine." Mother was hoping he'd accept her offer; it would make things easier. Also, while Mother's intellect told her heart not to be influenced by rugged good looks, her heart often told her intellect to "stuff it."

He glared at her silently. He not only didn't like her, but didn't even want to like her.

"No, then." She started to leave. "Then get your posse together and happy trails to you!" Mother had read enough American dime-novel Westerns to know the lingo.

Ian, just as Tasha was certain he would, barked, "Hold on!" His tone softened, "All right ... I know who you are and what folks say you can do, but I'm trail-boss here, ma'am. Know that!"

Tasha nodded and handed him the dart. "Boss ... please have this analysed and see if you can identify the girl. I'll pursue my own little errands and meet you here this afternoon." Ian was about to explode, but Mother warmly shook his hand. "I'm sure we'll get on famously, Ian."

He scowled at her. She patted the face of the grotesquely grinning corpse. "Keep smiling," she said cheerfully and then, collecting her unopened parasol from a nearby table, strode out of the bar.

Ian gritted his teeth then frowned at the dart. He handed it to Blake. "Well ... take it! See if the local doctor can find out what it is."

"Just like the lady said, sir?"

Ian growled and nodded.

CHAPTER FIFTEEN

Millport Island Woods

Mother trod a snaking path through the lush woods when she came to a fork in the road. She pressed a button on her parasol. The end of the handle flipped open revealing a compass inside. She picked the path on the right, strode on, and soon emerged into a clearing. Facing her on the other side of the small field was another ancient shrine, in the twisted form of a great, gnarled oak tree. Just visible through the overgrown moss and vines was an agonized face carved into its trunk, much like the ruins at McGloury's croft.

Mother stepped closer to investigate, treading though a path of leaves and shrubs. Suddenly a voice cried out, "Stop there, lassie!"

She peered into the forest, following the voice, and in the shadows saw someone hurrying toward her. She took a step in his direction when he shouted in haste, "Dinnae you move!" A ratty-looking grub of a man, wearing a seedy Tam-o'-shanter and carrying a heavy shotgun, walked into the light. He knelt down, keeping his eyes on Mother. He picked up a thick fallen branch and tossed it to her feet. The ground exploded as the jaws of a trap, meant for small game, shut, clutching the branch in an iron grip.

He grinned at her. "Now that would have been one well-turned ankle."

Mother gave him one of her penetrating and examining gazes as he set down his shotgun and reset his trap. She noticed his ragged attire, calloused and scarred hands, pale skin, ruddy nose, furtive movements, and his continually darting eyes. They told her quite a story.

She shook her head. "Poaching so soon after your release from prison is an exceedingly risky line of business."

Alarmed, he reached for his gun, but Tasha was faster and snatched it from his grasp, adding, "You'd find you had a firmer grip if you consumed less alcohol."

He narrowed his eyes at her cagily. "How long have you been spying on me."

"I've never laid eyes on you, Mister …?

"MacMurdo. What do you want?"

"Why not let me ask the questions? This is Laird MacGregor's property?"

MacMurdo gnashed his teeth then grudgingly nodded. "Aye. And it's prison again if he finds me on it."

"An occupational hazard of poaching. What is that tree?"

MacMurdo shrugged. "That?" He gave dismissive laugh. "Just an old cult shrine. We've got 'em thicker than my mother's porridge." Then he returned to more pressing matters. "Please let me go. I wouldna' survive another stretch from the Assizes."

"I'll forget I ever saw you for two favors."

He scowled at her suspiciously. "Go on."

"First, keep your eyes open and report to me anything unusual you see at night. I'm sure a poacher can do good work after dark."

"You said two favors."

She handed him back the shotgun. "Show me the way to Laird MacGregor's. I'm lost."

MacMurdo levelled the gun at her. "Aye, good and lost. Step into the trap."

"Manners," she warned him sternly.

"*Please* step into the trap," he repeated with a grin.

Mother nodded graciously, stepped toward the trap, stopped and asked, "Which foot?"

He didn't see the humour and brandished the weapon. Tasha moved one foot closer to the trap and then, with a fluid movement, kicked in a section of the branch MacMurdo had used earlier, springing the trap again. Before MacMurdo could recover his surprise, she reached over and once more pulled the shotgun from his hands.

"Did you know that thirty-four percent of released convicts never profit from their past mistakes?" She lunged toward him. The startled man jumped backward and tripped over a branch to fall backward to the earth. Mother offered her hand to help him up.

"Do we have an agreement, Mr. MacMurdo?"

He grasped her hand and she pulled him to his feet, but didn't loosen her grip. "Shall we shake to seal the bargain?" Mother's circus background had given her a grip of iron, and the little man was instantly on his knees in pain.

"It's a bargain!" he cried.

Mother increased the pressure. MacMurdo felt the bones in his hand starting to bend as she asked sweetly, "Word of honour?"

"Aye. Anything you like!" he yelled in torment.

She let go, and he clutched his hand, gasping. Tasha cocked her head down the path. "Now don't take advantage of me just because I'm a woman."

"This way," he said as he guided her, touching his hand tenderly with his fingers and wincing.

As they followed the serpentine path, MacMurdo, wary, kept a constant vigil all around, uncomfortable forging deeper into the Laird's domain. Tasha asked MacMurdo how well he knew the Laird. The poacher gave a disparaging laugh. "Know him! You cannae know a stranger."

"Then he's not an islander?" asked Mother.

"He was born here, that's true enough, but the man's practically a Sassenach. He didnae stay long, public school, life of a toff, couldnae care less about the crofters …"

"He was very concerned about Mr. McGloury stealing his sheep," observed Tasha.

MacMurdo snorted. "Pride! Just pride! As if he knew a dam from a mutton, or even cared, sitting high on his horse, proud as you please! It wasnae the sheep. It's what's his is his! His sort's all the same." MacMurdo gestured to the lush forest all around them, the greenest and most fecund part of the island. "You think this grand estate would miss the wee game caught in my traps? It's pride and greed!"

"The Laird returned to claim the estate when his father died?"

"And left again ... and then again ... he's a wanderer, that one. Mark me, I'll wager he couldnae put a name to more than ten faces on whole of this island."

They emerged around a curve in the path to a dirt road. MacMurdo pointed. "Just a wee bit that way. You'll pardon if I dinnae come along."

"Of course. Now remember to keep your part of the bargain."

She handed him back his shotgun. He instinctively grasped it with his hurt hand, grimaced at the weight, and hastily shifted hands, groaning. Tasha reached for his injured hand. MacMurdo promptly moved it away, but she was too fast and took his wrist, soothingly rubbed his hand. She gave his wrist a little squeeze. He grimaced and nodded as Mother blithely walked down the lane without looking back.

As Mother rounded the curve, she cleared the thick trees and spotted the manor. She marched to the front door of a huge, ancient, vine-covered pile that emerged from the surrounding forest, lifted the heavy iron knocker and let it fall against the massive door. She could hear the echoes from inside.

A husky butler opened the door. She handed him her card and he invited her in, leading her past a huge hearth with a blazing fire to a door in a dark hallway. "Wait here, please. I'll announce you."

She entered as the butler left, closing the door. Tasha examined the large room. The objects about her revealed that Laird MacGregor was manifestly a well-travelled man, for there were mementoes from all over the world on display.

One particular item drew Mother's interest. Mounted on the wall, above two matching sets of Japanese armour, were two South American Indian shields, and between them a blowgun.

Mother reached for the primitive weapon, but just as her fingers touched it, the door behind her opened. An attractive, but very stern woman in her forties walked in. She held Tasha's card in her hand and glared at Mother with almost manic intensity.

With no preamble or introduction, the woman said in a harsh voice: "Angus tells me you want to see my husband. What about?"

"I can discuss it only with your husband."

"You must be one of his London friends. What brass coming here."

"You are mistaken. I am here on business."

She flung the card at Mother. "You lying strumpet! Get out of here! You must think I've lost my wits, everyone on this fool island does. Do you suppose I've no eyes?" She suddenly yelled for the butler.

The hallway door began to open. Without taking her eyes off Mother, the woman announced, "This guttersnipe is leaving!"

The door fully opened and Laird MacGregor glowered into the study. "You're mistaken, Nessie. This lady's a friend of McGloury's."

Nessie didn't believe a word and sneered at Tasha. The Laird entered and said gently, "She's here on business." He put his hands on her shoulders and she wrenched away.

"Don't take me for a simpleton! You always liked them full," she said bitterly.

MacGregor glanced at the door and gave Angus, now present, an almost imperceptible nod. Tasha saw it, of course.

Angus cleared his throat. "Pardon, but your mother is asking for you."

Nessie glared at Tasha, then her focus wavered between Mother and the door, torn between leaving and remaining. MacGregor moved to her and said with tenderness, "You'd better see what she wants."

With a final glare at Tasha, Nessie silently glided out the room. Angus followed her out, closing the door quietly.

MacGregor turned his attention to Tasha. He stated, in a mixture of suspicion and embarrassment, "My wife is ... *eccentric*."

Tasha raised her eyebrows but took the chair he offered. MacGregor pointed to a decanter of port. She nodded and he poured drinks for them both.

He handed Mother her glass. "You will excuse me if I am blunt, Eliza ..."

"You may call me Tasha, Captain Crocker."

"So that's your game. Blackmail to keep my London life hidden."

"Do you believe that?"

He contemplated her over his glass in confusion. And then another reason suggested itself. His eyes twinkled; he put down his drink and placed his arms around Tasha. She gently pushed him away.

"We are not those people now," she said. "You are Laird of Millport Island."

"And you?"

"A private consulting detective."

He retrieved his drink and gave her a hard look. "What does McGloury want you to do?"

"You two seem to have differences."

"The man's a thief."

"And you desire his land?"

The Laird downed his drink to and refilled the glass. "I'll not deny that. I've been trying to purchase it for years. The older brother, Rupert, even agreed to sell it to me."

"I understand that the croft had been deserted for some time."

"Aye. Rupert lived in Glasgow."

"But you don't own it. What happened?"

The Laird scowled into his drink. "We had agreed on terms. My solicitors had sent Rupert the bill of sale to examine. Then the old man suddenly turned up here early, very early, one morning. It was storming and the passage must have been a rough one, but he came just the same. I'd never seen a man so terrified. He'd the fear of the devil in him. He ripped up the papers and refused to discuss it. But I was persistent. With that croft my land would reach the sea. I offered five times what it was worth. He finally consented. I was to go to Glasgow that Wednesday to settle the matter with his solicitor."

MacGregor poured another drink and began pacing the room. "I was told that the police found him, sitting dead in his study, a monstrous, sardonic grin on his face and his body stiff as stone. At his feet was the severed head of a goat ..." The excited gleam in Tasha's eyes made him stop.

She pressed her fingers together and leaned back. "So the croft passed to Rupert's younger brother. He now lives there and won't sell."

"The man's impossible. He doesn't know the first thing about sheep, except how to steal mine."

"I have heard that your neighbours hold a rather low opinion of your skills in that avocation."

The Laird bristled. "Perhaps I'm late in assuming my responsibilities, but I am assuming them now."

"Why now? I've heard you have very little attachment to Millport Island."

"It's my home ... and there comes a time in a man's life when that means more than perhaps it once did. So here I am. But we were discussing McGloury stealing my sheep."

Tasha shook her head. "You are not the only one around here losing sheep. So is McGloury, and that's only the beginning of his troubles."

The Laird sullenly glowered at Mother, then finally spoke. "And you think I've had a hand in it?"

"If anything happened to McGloury, what would happen to his land?"

"Depends on his will."

"If he died without leaving a will?"

"Well, I've heard he's the last of his clan. It would be put up at public auction."

"Sold to the highest bidder?"

He nodded.

"And who would the highest bidder on Millport Island be?" asked Tasha.

The Laird's face darkened and he took the glass from her hand. "I think you know that. I'll see you out."

Mother smiled, got up, but didn't move to the door. She circled the room glancing at the artefacts.

"You have a wonderful collection. Mostly weapons." She moved to the blowgun and took it from the wall, peering down the barrel. "Are you good with one?"

He took it from Mother. "It's only a decoration."

"Thank you for your time. As for Captain Crocker ..."

He studied her in apprehension, but Tasha added, "He knows a woman named Eliza. He has never met Tasha."

They didn't know it at the time, but Nessie was listening at the study door. She overheard her husband saying, "Thank you. Nessie has certain 'charms' that make an otherwise scandalous behaviour necessary for my sanity."

She stalked in fury to the staircase and climbed half way up, pausing to see her husband and Tasha emerge. MacGregor was still holding the blowgun as he led her to the front door. He opened the door and gave her a warning. "You'd better be careful of my boys. They haven't forgotten yesterday."

"Please speak with them so they don't have to remember today."

As he closed the door, MacGregor noticed Nessie descending the stairs glaring at him.

CHAPTER SIXTEEN

The Ruins

By mid-morning, Mother was at the ruins, examining the altar stone with her lens. She was now dressed in a long coat, cinched at the waist and set-off by an Inverness cape. She wore a sensible cap, almost masculine, but with a fore and aft brim that would shield from either sun or rain. A simple, almost stark, blouse and skirt, both designed by Mother, completed the ensemble, yet somehow on her, it all looked extremely smart. Above her loomed the rocky faces and the monolith with its great crescent-moon. A flock of seagulls alighted atop the various levels of the ruins and on the hard ground near Mother. Tasha knew that murder victims just didn't pop up out of the fog. They had to come from some-where.

And in that "somewhere" far below, Deirdre was gratified as, using her *camera obscura*, she watched Tasha's efforts. Sebastian, arms folded in displeasure, was watching, too. He started to speak, but Deirdre cut him off. "She knows that the girl must have come from somewhere, but she can't find any evidence to support the deduction."

Tasha, projected on the flat, polished tabletop, shook her head and leaned dejectedly against the ruins. Sebastian frowned in disapproval.

If Deirdre noticed, she didn't care. "We haven't heard from the look-outs this morning. Signal them."

"With her up top? She'll spot the messenger."

To Deirdre, Sebastian—in fact, sometimes everyone—could be so dense. He scowled.

"Temper, temper," she said soothingly.

"Why be a bloody fool?" That he cursed in front of a lady, even one as familiar to him as Deirdre, disclosed the degree of his apprehension.

Deirdre's eyes flared, as all traces of tenderness vanished. Sebastian stopped. He'd gone the limit and he knew it.

"You question your Priestess." Her ritualistic statement was void of emotion. Deidre motioned with her hand, turning the palm upward.

Sebastian, subdued, extended his hand, also palm up, and stepped to her. Deirdre placed her hand atop his and, expertly wielding the edge of her crescent-moon ring, sliced his skin. Sebastian did not react as blood pooled in his cupped palm. She gently anointed the red-pearl crescent in his blood, then extended her hand with the signet ring, now glistening red, toward Sebastian. He leaned forward and kissed the ring, stepped away, his lips wet with his own blood, and lowered his head as he intoned the required response:

"I am yours—always."

With that surrender, she slowly, mechanically, brushed her fingers across his hand. "Send the messenger."

Up above, Mother was still leaning thoughtfully against the rocks. Suddenly, the seagulls near her took flight, snapping away her contemplation. She tensed with interest as she spotted something. Tasha carefully removed her fore-and- aft hat, aimed, and tossed it.

The hat landed atop a carrier pigeon—the lone bird remaining on the ancient stones. Tasha delicately removed a rice-paper note from around the animal's leg and read the single word it contained: "Constant?"

"You're a cryptic little messenger, aren't you?" Mother said to the captive bird.

She glanced at the weather-worn granite near the altar stone, where she had captured the pigeon, and carefully studied the network of deep cracks, running her finger along one that caught her attention. She stood and gave a slight satisfied nod, then turned her attention back to the cooing bird in her hand.

She went to the cottage and was gratified to find a thick spool of string. Then, after getting her purse and parasol, tied a length of string to the bird's leg and secured the opposite end to the front door latch. She tossed the pigeon into the air and, once it settled on a direction, noted the heading by using the compass in the handle of her parasol.

CHAPTER SEVENTEEN

The Mainland

After a ferry crossing—the captain had grinned at the pigeon Tasha had carried in the wicker basket of Tom's "borrowed" bike—Tasha was on the mainland. She bicycled to the top of a hill, well away from the city, and released the bird. Now free of the string, its flight through the treetops guided Tasha, who took off in pursuit.

She almost lost the pigeon in a flock of other birds, but managed to keep him separate in her sights and continued the chase.

The pigeon flew into a hole atop the tower of an old ruined church situated high on the crest of a hill. Tasha dismounted the bicycle, examining the crumbling wreckage. The grounds were overgrown and the building showed the cankerous neglect of generations, likely centuries. Gaping holes punctured the stonework, and a tree grew in the roofless nave. The former house of worship was what would now be called "redundant," but at the time there was no official designation, merely abandonment and disrepair.

Then Tasha saw a bright flash of light from the tower window. She hurried inside. As she opened the side chapel door, it fell from its hinges, raising a thick cloud of dust. Dust covered the scattered remains of the few broken pews, some fallen stones, and the dull remnants of stained-glass windows. But visible in the dust were footprints leading to a door behind the altar, which opened to well-worn steps that led up into the tower.

Tasha, quietly as a cat, climbed the stairs, soon coming to a door set back in an alcove. This portal had been repaired recently, for one of the hinges was new. The door was ajar, so she used the chance to observe. From within she heard the cooing of pigeons. The far wall was covered with cages, half of them full. Her eyes glittered at this, and then she heard someone coming down the stairs.

Mother ducked inside a corner as a stocky man in a monk's robe, wearing neither cross nor other religious symbols, appeared. Holding Tasha's pigeon, he walked into the aviary and closed the door. Tasha, never one to refuse an invitation, climbed past and came to another door at the very top of the stairs. She listened, but heard no sound. She peeked through a crack in the doorframe.

Save for a telescope, the room was empty. Tasha entered— the flash she had seen must have been the sun flaring off the lens. She peered through the eyepiece, being careful not to jar the instrument.

The telescope was trained on the harbour, and there in the firth was the *Dreadnought*. She pondered the connection between the *Dreadnought* and these incidents—but there were too many missing links in this chain. Mother preferred to wait for facts before drawing conclusions.

As Tasha left the church, she was watched by the monk, who hid behind a dusty tapestry.

When she had peddled out of sight of the church, the monk tossed another pigeon, a message secured on its leg, into flight.

Chapter Eighteen

Millport Island Ferry

asha, lost in thought, stood in the bow of the little steam ferryboat. The captain lashed the wheel, walked up behind her, and noted the empty wicker basket. "Lose the bird?"

"Flew the coop."

The boat heaved as the swells increased in strength and icy spray inundated both of them. The captain watched the darkening sky. "There's a braw squall blowin' in. You'll not find me, nor anyone with sense, on the water."

"I'd have thought an old salt like you could weather a few waves."

He gave a quick snort, "You go on thinking that." He pointed toward the mainland. "Me, I'll be home in a dry bed with a wet whisky. Sorry if the storm sets back your studies, lass."

Mother wasn't sure what he meant by "studies," but the strange reference sounded promising. She gestured for him to continue.

"Are you not one of these students, then?" the captain asked as he spat tobacco over the side.

"What is so educational about Millport Island?"

"The ruins, of course. Every so often some Sassenach student of history comes here hoping to be the lucky one ... but you're nae student." He sauntered back to the wheel and, as he expected, Tasha followed, intrigued.

"Oh, I study everything. You really should have the gas turned back on in your house, Captain."

"How did you …?" he gasped in surprise.

The initiative was now Tasha's. "You first … 'be the lucky one'?"

"… the lucky one who finds the lost cult refuge, the one in the legend." The old salt stopped, his eyes twinkling. Tasha waited, then the expected happened as the ferry captain scratched his head and said, "I cannae recall more, lass. My memory's wandered."

Tasha had already retrieved a gold sovereign from her purse. Without changing expression, she flipped the coin to him. "Your 'legend' had better be more original than your approach."

The captain gave a crooked grin, pocketed the sovereign and began. "Aye. It's a long tale, I might miss a few details …"

She closed her purse and folded her arms. That settled the matter.

"… but not too many," the ferry captain admitted in defeat. "A thousand years back, all the land around the firth was the stronghold of a pagan cult. Legend says they had a name—but all I know is 'Olc'!'"

Tasha raised her eyebrows questioningly.

"It means wicked. Now, maybe they had other names; ask the islanders. But I do know this: Their priestess ruled with an iron hand, and if she marked a man for death, that was the finish of him. The poor wretch might try to flee ... hide ..." The captain mournfully shook his head. "There is no night so black, no chamber so concealed to hide a mortal from the powers of the dark priestess. The light of dawn would find her prey, his face a hideous death grin, his skin as tight and rigid as oak. And then ..."

Tasha perked up, intensely interested. The captain stopped his story. "Aye, the rest eludes me."

She reached into her purse and out came another coin. She held it out of reach with the warning, "Remember, they hang pirates."

He beamed and tapped his head. "The fog's clearin'. Well, it went on like that until the Christians, bless 'em, came. The cult fought like the very devil, but they couldnae win. They fled to a secret refuge on Millport Island and no one could find them. Not until ... oh ... ah ..."

Tasha, started to replace the coin in her purse.

The captain hurriedly added, "... until one of their own betrayed the cult for gold. They were slaughtered to the last believer and their priestess was burned at the stake as a witch. Before she died, she cursed all Christians and vowed revenge. Revenge on the island clan that betrayed her. Revenge on the entire Christian world that destroyed her. Revenge to the very end of forever."

"And the location of this secret refuge?"

"Lost." He shook his head. "Time, lass, it buries everything."

Tasha handed "Jolly Jack Tar" the coin. "Does it? Revenge to the end of forever ..." She leaned on the rail, absorbed, fingers and palms in a thoughtful pyramid.

CHAPTER NINETEEN

London, The Admiralty

At the same time Mother was questioning the ferry captain, there was a meeting in the Admiralty's venerable boardroom. In this room, the Royal Navy had directed its fight against Napoleon, had seen England's wooden walls replaced with steel and steam. Today, there was plenty of gold braid sitting around the conference table, as well as lesser beings, like Commander Bernard, and several civilians in dark frockcoats and wing-collars, among them Ramsgate and Mycroft Holmes.

Mycroft was staring at the front page of the *London Times*. Its headline: "Berlin denies the *Dreadnought* charges. Debate in Commons."

Ramsgate was concluding, "… the missing plans have not yet reached Germany. Our sources are certain on that point."

"We know where the plans *aren't*, Commissioner," said Mycroft testily as he softly put down the newspaper.

"I assure you, Mr. Holmes, every available man …"

"Available man?" interrupted Mycroft. "Every man! Forget your petty problems of the police court. There can be no further incidents involving the *Dreadnought*, gentlemen, or all Europe will have war!"

His words hung heavily in the air. Mycroft Holmes was not a man given to hyperbole.

CHAPTER TWENTY

Millport Village

Tasha leaned against the counter of the telegraph office, which was merely a piece of plank at the back of a small general goods store/post office, and filled out a telegraph form:

"Ramsgate, having wonderful time, scenery fascinating. Especially view of your boat. There are other interested parties here. Will keep you informed. Tasha."

She gave the form to an old woman behind the counter who was knitting a shawl that seemed to extend yards behind her. "You've been at that a long time," commented Tasha cheerily.

"Aye," came the curt reply.

"I don't imagine that a place like Millport keeps the wires very busy."

"We have no wires. We use a semaphore," she said, not looking up from her knitting.

"What do you do during fog?" asked Tasha, intrigued.

The old woman lowered her knitting and took the form. "We wait till it lifts." She read over the message and vanished into a back room. Tasha flipped a coin to the counter and reached for another, only to discover to her chagrin that the cupboard was bare. The "pirate" captain had ravaged her coin purse better than she knew.

As Mother left the "telegraph office," she noticed Alec and Sean watching from across the street. They tried not to be conspicuous.

Tasha walked down the cobble-stoned street, aware of them, when she heard a gunshot. With feline quickness, she flattened herself against the corner of a building. No one else on the street, including Alec and Sean, seemed aware of the shot; from the baker taking a basket of bread to the pub to the two fishwives gossiping in front of the green-grocer, it was business as usual on High Street.

Comprehension dawned upon Tasha as her vigilance travelled to the telegraph office. In the sky was a signal flare, fired by the old woman, now on the roof, holding a smoking flare-gun. The flare burned brightly for the sky was dark with storm clouds. The old woman peered through a telescope to the opposite shore. She must have seen an answering signal of some kind, for she grasped the control wheels of a strange apparatus. It was a pole that extended twenty feet into the sky. There was an eight-foot arm at the top and another identical one about half way down the main shaft. Both of the arms were connected to the main shaft with pivots. The device, a Popham semaphore, was archaic even then. The old woman deftly worked the control wheels. The semaphore arms twirled rapidly as they sent Tasha's message. Mother watched in fascination for half a minute, and then continued down the street.

She noted out of the corner of her eye that Alec (the bigger man) had moved to follow her, but after a few steps his smaller companion held him back. What she didn't hear was Sean telling Alec, "We know where to find the little Sassenach when we want her."

Tasha walked on. Suddenly she stopped, for right in the middle of the street was a huge oak tree. There were benches around it, and carved on the trunk, facing her, was another of the brutal faces. This one was better preserved than the one she had seen earlier in the forest. On a low brick ledge around the base of the tree was a brass faceplate with the inscription: "Ceremonial Tree—Preserved through the Millport Island Historical Society."

A shadow loomed over the faceplate; it was the old woman from the telegraph office. "You could not have a reply already," stated Mother.

"No. A message. MacMurdo the poacher wants to see you."

"Do you know where I can ..."

"The pub. He's in the Spotted Dog."

That was true, for it was in the Spotted Dog that Mother spotted MacMurdo at a table in the corner. He raised his glass to her. Also in the pub were Sean and Alec. They stopped playing darts and nodded gleefully to each other as Tasha walked in.

The men in the place fell silent and glared at her for invading their masculine sanctuary. She gave the assembly her most charming smile. Mother rather enjoyed her assaults on what today we'd call chauvinism, or outright discrimination, and trod through the pub as if she owned it. She was striding toward MacMurdo in the back of the room, when a dart flew past her face and embedded itself in the wall. Alec, another dart in hand, grinned at Tasha with the kind of nasty smirk best to stay friendly with. Tasha mischievously wagged her finger and reached to remove the dart from the wall when another landed less than an inch from her fingers. The men in the pub laughed.

Alec, still grinning, shouted at her, "Do you play, lass?"

"No," said Mother in a pleasant and agreeable tone, "but it doesn't look difficult." She pulled both darts from the wall, spun and threw them in the same liquid movement.

Alec ducked and when he raised his head it was bare. His ghillie hat was affixed to the dartboard behind him, secured directly to the bulls-eye by one dart, while the second missile was stuck squarely in the tail of the first.

Tasha gave a playful grin. "Think what I could do with practice." This sobering thought allowed her to stride past the troublemakers. She stopped, took the pint of beer from Alec's hand, drained it in one swig, and returned the empty glass.

A few men laughed, liking her nerve, but the prevailing attitude was hostile and—with glares from the others—silence was soon restored. By that time, Tasha was at MacMurdo's table. She caught the eye of the Publican. "Whisky. A hauf! I always prefer the local product."

She then turned her attention to MacMurdo and asked, "Has my little ferret turned up something important?"

"Aye. Very!"

She motioned him to continue. He noted his dry throat.

Mother replied in mock-sympathy. "Would a glass of scotch whisky help to lubricate your tonsils?"

He gave a toothy grin. Mother continued, "The faster you speak, the sooner you'll have it." His grin foundered.

"I dinnae like your attitude, lass, not one bit. And after I've decided to trust you."

"It's more pleasant than prison."

MacMurdo was palpably in his cups and rose unsteadily to his feet. "Ye got no respect, woman!"

She took his hand in hers and gave a little squeeze. He instantly sat down and she let go. "I would have thought a poacher would be wiser in the art of discretion. You have picked a singularly public spot for our private conversation. The Spotted Dog has keen ears."

MacMurdo shifted his bleary vision around the room. There were many eyes on them, including Alec and Sean.

Tasha tilted her head toward the door. "Let's talk outside. The natives are restless."

Alec, with an effort, freed his hat from the dartboard, and with Sean, followed the Publican as he brought Tasha her whisky. They flanked either side of her as Tasha, cagily, started to stand. Alec put his big hands on her shoulders and, with more effort than he expected, forced her down.

"If you prefer the men's section, Sassenach, then bide awhile." He gave a quick, and entirely humourless, laugh.

MacMurdo grinned. "You've a gift for makin' friends, lass."

Alec glared at MacMurdo. "When we've finished with this little strumpet, MacMurdo ..." MacMurdo sunk back in his chair, discernibly frightened.

Tasha shook her head patiently.

"Sneering city lass," joined in Sean. "The woman and children's room wasn't grand enough for her likes. She has to peep and pry on the men."

Tasha was about to comment when she spotted a crescent-moon tattoo on Alec's wrist. Sean and Alec exchanged worried looks. Sean pulled Tasha to her feet, "We'll take you there, lass."

Tasha shook free and straightened her clothes, "Ah, an escort, how very ..." Her elbow lanced into Sean's stomach, as he doubled over, her fist connected with his jaw. He flew back, smashing his head against the bar, and stayed put, lights out, on the floor. Tasha, having barely moved, continued to adjust her clothes, "... chivalrous."

Everyone in the pub was stunned. Alec attacked. As he threw a blow, Tasha picked up her glass of whisky and dodged his every effort without spilling a drop. Then she tossed the drink in Alec's face.

"Have one on me." She just could not resist. Her fist smashed into Alec's jaw. He crashed through a table, hurtled to the floor, and slowly staggered back to his feet. He looked bleary-eyed at Tasha.

Mother swiftly moved to MacMurdo and asked him, "Quickly! What did you want to tell me?"

"I know who's been stealing the Laird's sheep. It's Leprechauns!"

"Leprechauns! In modern Scotland?"

Before MacMurdo could say more, he motioned for Tasha to glance behind. Alec, in a fury, lunged toward her.

Mother assumed the classic Marquis of Queensbury pugilistic stance and thumbed the side of her nose.

At the front door, Ian and Blake entered. "I'll stop the fight, sir," said Blake.

"What fight?" answered Ian, holding him back.

Alec threw punch after punch, but Tasha, hands on hips, dodged every one of them while giving her opponent useful pugilistic tips. "You really must work on speed. And remember ... always ... keep ... aware ... of your opponent!" Her foot connected squarely with Alec's jaw. He sailed into a group of onlookers, who broke his fall. He stood—showing either admirable stamina or a streak of masochism—smashed a bottle on the bar and brandished it. "I'll fix your face for you!" he growled. Even to this day, when a Scot offers to fix your face for you, be assured he is not a doctor offering free plastic surgery.

At this point, the very reluctant Ian pointed Blake toward the fight and barked, "Oh, go on!"

With all interest on Tasha no one saw Sean, now back on his feet, take a knife from his coat and inflict a slight nick on MacMurdo's wrist. MacMurdo didn't seem to feel it.

Blake moved in, but he wasn't needed. Tasha dodged Alec's lunge, planted her elbow in his passing back, and decked him. He dropped the shattered bottle, then smashed into Sean, who was racing toward Tasha from MacMurdo's table. She turned around and plucked a drink from the hands of an on-looker.

Mother turned back, raised her glass in bravado, and toasted the defeated men. "The best laid schemes o' mice and men gang aft agley."

Mother had recited Robert Burns original version of the famous phrase and many of the men, despite Tasha being a "Sassenach," appreciated the authentic quote. They also fairly applauded her skill and victory. Mother gave a grateful nod. She was fond of Scots. Despite Harry Lauder's popular music-hall presentation depicting them as flint-eyed and tight-fisted, she found most Scots to be a warm and generous people.

Alec picked himself off the floor and staggered to the bar, clutching it for support. Sean started to get up and reached for his knife when he spotted a streak of blood on his hand. He picked up the knife; there was a thin smear of his blood on the blade. Sean realised that he must have cut himself in the fall and was horrified.

Tasha sensed something was wrong and offered her hand in assistance. Sean reached for it, started to choke, dropped his hand, and collapsed to the floor. He was quite dead.

Mother took a step toward him when a hand grasped her arm. On reflex, she pivoted and punched her assailant. It was Ian, who she sent sprawling, unconscious, to the ground. Tasha spotted her error. "I've been rude." She poured a whisky, bent down and gently slapped Ian's face.

Alec used the distraction to slip away unnoticed.

Ian's eyes dragged open and Tasha tenderly put the drink to his lips. He shoved it away and fingered his throbbing jaw. Tasha, ignoring his silent protest, helped him up. "I do so apologize."

"Is this women's emancipation?" He spotted Sean on the floor, "Always havin' men at your feet?"

"I thought you were attacking me."

"I ain't that reckless."

She chuckled at that. He softened a bit and the ice between them began to thaw. "We may smoke a peace-pipe yet, Sheriff," noted Tasha (secretly delighted at the thought and not just for professional reasons).

"Inspector," he corrected her—but there was a glint of humour in his voice.

Tasha knelt down to Sean. "Have you ever been tattooed, Inspector?" She pointed to the crescent-moon on Sean's wrist.

Ian was confused. He noted Sean's very slight wound. "But that's just a scratch."

"Poisoned—like our little blonde beauty."

Out came Ian's official notebook—and official attitude. "I'll need statements from you and the other tin-horn you were tusslin' with." He scanned the room for Alec. "Blake, find where he skedaddled off to, and then send for the sawbones."

Blake nodded and left. Tasha pointed to Sean. "I think this fellow's beyond help."

"You're the one partial to autopsies, ain't you, ma'am?"

Mother appreciated his concession. "Tasha will do. We already know one thing about his death ..." She turned over the body, revealing Sean's face. He was grinning from ear-to-ear. "He died happy." She gestured toward MacMurdo and added, "He was not alone."

MacMurdo sat rigidly in his seat, staring at them with the same distorted grin.

"He was about to give me information. This was deliberate. I suspect there was more to this brawl than a clash of personalities. I think it's time for a little pow-wow."

Later in the day, much to the chagrin of both the Publican and his clientele, Ian emptied the pub. Sean and MacMurdo's bodies, now on tables, were covered with horse-blankets. Constable Blake had returned, unable to find the doctor, who was attending a patient on another part of the island. The constable had left word that the physician was needed at the pub and returned to the Spotted Dog to report. Blake now sat in a corner, watching Ian refer to his notes while deeply in conversation with Tasha.

"You over-think things." Ian tapped his notebook with his finger. "I got one creed that hits pay-dirt every time. I always track down a motive, and we both know where that trail leads. There's only one varmint who wants McGloury's land."

"Laird MacGregor?" said Mother doubtfully.

"You have objections?"

"One or two. Why would he kill McGloury's brother after he had agreed to sell him the croft?"

"We've only his word on that."

Tasha shook her head, "It's too easily checked for it to be a fabrication."

Ian put down his notebook, filled a glass from a bottle of (non-alcoholic) Iron Brew on the table, and said evenly, "As far as I can see, there's no one else with a motive."

"You must extend your horizon, Inspector. There is someone else. With time I will prove it."

"Maybe … but what I say goes." Ian motioned to the constable in the corner. "Blake, stay here and wait for the doctor!" He pointed to the two dead bodies. "I want to know what killed those men." Ian shifted his extended finger to Mother. "Meanwhile, we're going to pay Laird MacGregor a visit!"

CHAPTER TWENTY-ONE

The Caverns, Deirdre's Chamber

The chamber was filled with the sound of the old ballad "Barbara Allen" being flawlessly played on a harp. Von Traeger, in fencer's regalia, dueled with another man, also in protective gear—though "dueling" might be an overstatement. The German gained easy ground, forcing his opponent to the wall and then disarmed him with a deft lunge. Another flick of the wrist and the straps of the cornered man's protective mask were severed. It fell away revealing a terrified Alec. Von Traeger, enjoying himself, toyed with his victim, slashing Alec's arms and laughing at the man's panic. The wounds were deliberately superficial, but Alec whimpered, watching the red stains spread on his white sleeves. He tried to fight down his growing dread.

Von Traeger was pleased as he lectured, "In Heidelberg, we fight mensur style. The target is the head." And his cheek bore the dueling scar that was a mark of pride with the Prussian aristocracy.

"My men use their heads occasionally," interrupted Deirdre, who wore her priestess robes while playing her ornate harp. She stopped; her nimble fingers left the strings. Her remorseful voice was almost motherly. "But not you, Alec. You and Sean were sent to observe Lady Dorrington. Not only did you disobey me by attacking her, but you let her win."

Von Traeger snapped the point of his blade under Alec's chin, not breaking the skin, but forcing Alec to his toes. Alec gaped pleadingly at Deirdre.

Her fingers floated across the strings, producing an eerie dissonance. "You and Sean have nearly upset a delicately balanced equation." Deirdre plucked the harp. The sound was dark and angry. "Lady Dorrington must have her clues in the proper sequence." Her voice became vehement. "I'm leading our little detective to the greatest crime in history. Holding it in front of her eyes, and yet she can't see it." Deirdre suddenly stopped.

Alec and Von Traeger were amazed at her intensity. The blade dropped from Alec's chin. He breathed hard in relief. "MacMurdo the poacher was about to talk. We stopped him."

Deirdre's fires died as rapidly as they flared. She returned to her harp and continued matter-of-factly. "He would have said nothing she doesn't already suspect, but cannot prove." She plucked the cords and said sadly, "I can't risk unpredictable elements, Alec."

Alec was terrified, but not stupid, and he knew what that meant. He bolted past Von Traeger and threw himself at Deirdre's feet, grasping the hem of her robe. "Please, Priestess—forgive me. This Sassenach woman—she's destroying you … and we need you so … we …" He ceased talking and offered his palm for the blood supplication.

"Not that way, Alec," she said softly, as she helped him to his feet and embraced him.

"Priestess, please." Alec desperately pleaded for forgiveness. Her embrace suddenly tightened and her fingernails dug deeply into his neck. He tensed, looked at her in anguish, and then quivered in her arms. She loosened her caress and he reached for the wounds, feeling the wet blood. His eyes darted from his stained fingers to his priestess. Deirdre gave him a kiss on the forehead. "You have violated one of our most ancient and unviable rules: I alone decide the Smiling Death." He slid down her body to the floor.

"Yes, Alec. Forgiven," she took a towel from the table and wiped the lethal poison from her nails.

Von Traeger angrily marched over, "Even a *dummer mensch* deserves a decent death!"

"He looks contented enough."

Alec's corpse grinned with the cult's gruesome trademark. Deirdre sat back at the harp and resumed "Barbara Allen," singing with the voice of an angel. She was capable of much beauty.

Von Traeger and two men carried Alec's stiff, grinning body into a bizarre chamber that was almost completely carved with the brutal faces visible on the ruins above. Very little of the natural rock had been left uncleaved. The most elaborate work was the floor, where an agonized face, with a mammoth open mouth, gaped frozen in an eternal silent scream. Ruby crystals were set deep in the eye-sockets of the floor's visage, gleaming crimson and reflecting the torches that were fixed to the wall. These torches jutted out of the eyes of the wall carvings, suggesting they had been blinded by impalement. Surrounded by the tortured faces, the chamber embodied unceasing torment.

Von Traeger snapped his fingers, and Alec's body was dumped into the maw on the ground. The corpse vanished into the blackness, but there was no sound of impact. Von Traeger stared into the endless darkness. "Odd how you never hear them hit bottom."

Chapter Twenty-two

Laird MacGregor's Manor

Tasha and Ian travelled by gig (the one-horse cart was Ian's official conveyance on the island) to the Laird's manor. The sky had darkened, and a rising wind now bent the trees.

There was already a small, black carriage by the front door. The Laird evidently had another visitor. Tasha beheld the unexpected gig in concern and told Ian to hurry. They both rushed to the door, which was opened by Angus. Tasha noted he was unshaven and his uniform was disheveled, but there was something else. Angus's demeanour had not the impassive formality of a gentleman's gentleman, but a man fighting for self-control. On a small island like Millport, nearly everyone recognised Ian. Angus stammered, "We … we weren't expecting the authorities so promptly, sir."

Tasha brushed past him. "It's the Laird, isn't it?"

Angus could only manage a weak nod. Ian quizzically stared at Mother, who kept her eyes on Angus and asked, in a softening tone, "How bad?"

Angus seemed incapable of speech—his mouth opened wordlessly as he searched desperately around. Then, in relief, Angus spotted the old doctor at the top of the stairs with a Cammann binaural stethoscope, looking very much like its modern counterpart, around his neck.

"Well, I think we've found out why Constable Blake couldn't locate the good doctor to perform the autopsies," said Tasha as she hurried up the stairs and asked again, "How bad?" The physician eyed her blankly and then placed the stethoscope in his ears.

"I'm a wee bit hard of hearing, lass." He held out the stethoscope for her, while Ian came up behind them. The doctor addressed him, "It's an ugly business, Inspector. I just sent the lad for you. How did you find out?"

Ian impatiently took the stethoscope from Tasha's hands and spoke into it. "Find out what?"

"That the Laird's wife tried to murder him," responded Tasha evenly.

"Please, let me handle this!" Ian snapped his head back toward the doctor, who replied in a very loud voice, "The Laird's wife attempted to murder him."

Ian cast a mean glare at Mother, who enjoyed it, "People on this island have peculiar pastimes."

The doctor shook his head grimly and boomed, "The Laird's alive … for now. Nessie, Lady MacGregor, is quiet."

The three of them silently entered Nessie's room. She sat in a high-backed chair, her eyes manically focused on the floor. An elderly maid was nervously in her Lady's attendance.

"Mother knew all along," hissed Nessie, her unblinking gaze riveted to the floor. Then slowly, she shifted her notice to the people in the doorway. At the sight of Tasha, she flew from her chair in a sudden spasm of rage. "You! It was you! I knew it was!" She collided with Tasha, wrapping her fingers around her throat. "Slut! Mother said it would be you!"

Tasha easily raised her arms, breaking Nessie's chokehold. Ian tried to grasp her, but Nessie broke free and bolted out the door, fleeing down the hall.

"Are you hurt?" Ian asked Tasha in concern.

She shook her head. "I'm used to tantrums. I'm a mother."

The doctor prepared a hypo from his black bag. "If you can catch her, this'll quiet her down."

Ian was ready for action, "We'll search the place."

"That won't be necessary," Mother replied quietly.

Ian, about to argue, cut himself short as he noted Tasha's focus was on the doorway. Angus stood there, seemingly having recovered his professional formality. "I can take you to her. This way, please."

The bedroom door was open. Angus stood back as Tasha, Ian, and the doctor, his syringe ready, peered inside. The boudoir, though old fashioned, was elegant. Nessie knelt at an ornate four-poster bed, talking to someone hidden by the thick bed-curtains that draped from above. Her words were confessional, but there was an underlying pleading, as if seeking approval. "I did just what you told me to do, Mother. I waited; I watched and bided my time. I caught him, just the way you promised."

Tasha made a signal and the trio silently entered, circling either side of the distracted woman. At once, Tasha and Ian grasped each of Nessie's arms and pulled her away from the bed.

She struggled, crying for her mother, shrieking that the men were trying to kill her. The old doctor plunged the syringe into Nessie's arm and presently she became docile; her head dropped and her voice shriveled to an almost indistinct mumble, "They're trying to kill me!"

As Nessie became a dead weight in their arms, Tasha and Ian moved her to the bed, pushing away the curtains. There, propped against the headboard, exquisitely dressed in a silk night robe, was a startlingly real wax figure of an older woman who bore a resemblance to Nessie.

"Mother?" mused Tasha to Angus, now entering the room.

Angus nodded. "Yes, ma'am. The Laird had it made by Madame Tussauds from her death mask."

"I take it mother and daughter were close?" asked Tasha with a nod toward Nessie, "and she reacted strongly to her Mother's passing."

"She never accepted the loss, ma'am. Her moods became darker."

Tasha nodded and, displaying no emotion for the pathetic creature in their arms, merely said, "Let's not have her wake up in her mother's bed."

Angus led them to Nessie's room.

Mother, Ian, and the doctor warmed themselves before the hearth in the Laird's study. The doctor, still wearing his stethoscope, reached into his black bag as he explained, "Nessie suspected the Laird of wenching. When he returned home, she attacked him with this." He pulled a dart from the Laird's blowgun from his bag. "There was no poison on the dart, but it landed near his heart."

Ian, who was writing the facts down in his notebook, asked, "What are his chances?"

The doctor only stared silently, until Tasha repeated the question into the stethoscope. The doctor responded with a shrug. Then he gave Mother a stern look. "She suspected that her husband was seeing you, lassie."

"Poor woman. Mad as a hatter," Mother replied pleasantly into the stethoscope.

The doctor squinted flinty eyes at her.

Angus silently entered, bearing a tray of tea. Ian told the doctor that he was needed on pressing police business back at the pub and assured Angus that Constable Blake would be sent to take Nessie into custody.

"I take it the Laird is no longer a suspect?" Mother asked Ian.

"You know, you're as subtle as a stampede," he growled as he strode to the door.

Outside the windows was the pitter-patter of rain.

CHAPTER TWENTY-THREE

Millport Village

The long-brewing storm had arrived at last. Lightning flashed in the window of the pub, and Ian, hearing the rain smashing against the glass and the wail of the wind, took note of the tempest's severity. He was focusing on the weather as a respite from his argument with Tasha. She sat at a table in the otherwise deserted pub.

At last he turned from the window and shook his head, "Sorry, no." Mother started to protest, but Ian raised his hand and continued. He couldn't mask the mocking quality in his voice. "Excavate the ruins on Mr. McGloury's farm! Dig up a historical treasure on the say-so of some local yarn the ferry captain spun for you!"

"Local yarns may be embellished, but they always have a solid centre of fact."

"Real? Like that 'banshee' you said you saw?"

"I said I saw someone trying to frighten Mr. McGloury by impersonating one."

"You also said that this here goblin left no footprints ...."

"She stood on stone, there are not always marks."

"And then it just up and ..." Ian snapped his fingers. "Vamoosed like smoke!"

"There is a well-hidden entrance to some chamber beneath those ruins."

"How do you know?" Ian asked with a short laugh.

"Because it must be so."

Ian shook his head in exasperation. "It was foggy, it—she—could've just skedaddled off."

"Then there would be footprints. There were none. There is also a crack in the stones, very deep and free of accumulated dirt and home to neither insects nor shrubs. In short, a concealed entrance, used recently and no doubt controlled from within."

Ian shrugged, but before he could speak ... "The cult *must* be under there and I will find the way in," Tasha said with asperity rising in her voice.

"Ancient cults! Old curses!" Ian flipped shut his notebook. "I can just see handin' in a report like that. They think I'm kinda loco at the station as it is."

"Three singularly contented corpses should be conspicuous enough for even the official force." Mother could spew sarcasm with the best of them. "There is also the connection between the tattoo on my assailant's arm and the design at the ruins."

"Everyone in these parts knows those marks—folks here grew up with 'em."

"Do 'folks here' usually die from a death-grin poison? Have you seen reports of any similar deaths in the last several months?"

Ian thought for a moment. "There was one."

Tasha leaned in closer. "McGloury's older brother Rupert?"

Ian was startled, his eyes locked on Mother. He contemplated her words then slowly nodded.

Mother quickly continued, "Shall I draw you a picture, Inspector? Every instance of these gruesome demises has been connected with this island and in some way with McGloury's croft. Rupert died that way—preventing him from selling the croft to the Laird, forcing it to remain in the McGloury family and luring my client back here."

"What for?" shot back Ian. "What'd they—if there is a *they*—want?"

"I have several theories ..."

"Theories!" he said disparagingly. "Look, just because the Laird's crazy wife tried to do him in, doesn't clear him with me. He's got a motive! It's real, not a campfire tale."

"There is something buried deeply here, Inspector. This has scope. There is the work of an artist here, and one with an almost feminine sensitivity."

"The trail leads back to motive. The Laird—"

"The Laird doesn't have this kind of imagination," interrupted Tasha. Her thoughts went back to "Captain Crocker" at the Inn of Illusion. "Take my word for it."

Ian walked over to her and pulled out a chair, took a deep breath and said quietly, "Tasha, people kick off all the time without dead religions doin' the kickin'! Now I gotta admit that it's one humdinger of a story, but this ain't no storybook country. Glasgow's just up the firth. And anyway, what about this church with that monk ..."

"Not a monk. He wore no cross and the church is an unused ruin."

"Well, whoever the varmints are, you say they're spyin' on the *Dreadnought*? How does that fit in?"

"How indeed?" was all she'd offer in answer.

He waited for her to continue—but she didn't. Mother had stated her case. Repetition, which some men called "nagging," was not her forte.

Ian raised his hands in a gesture of confusion. "Sorry, but if I'm gonna look like a tenderfoot to my boss, it's gonna be on more evidence than some old salt's fable."

"I have only shared this much because I need help from the official force to connect the links of my chain."

"You dig up some evidence I can use and you'll get it!"

"If we 'dig up' the ruins you'll have it."

The back-room door opened and the doctor entered.

In his massive voice, he replied, "Aye! It's the same wicked poison that killed the wee lassie this morning. I dinnae suppose you'd care to confide what it is?"

"I was hopin' you'd know," replied Ian.

The doctor waved him off. "It's nae good, I cannae hear you."

Ian opened his mouth for another effort, but Tasha took the stethoscope, put it in the doctor's ear and said softly. "We don't know."

The doctor gave a short laugh. "That wasnae worth hearing." He tipped his hat and shambled off, when Tasha, still holding the stethoscope, pulled him back and asked, "I want to see the local records, as far back as they go. Especially anything relating to your ancient and infamous cult. Where are they?"

The doctor answered at once, "In the Historical Society, of course. But it isnae open after two." He pulled the stethoscope from her and retreated. She cut him off, and once more, spoke into the stethoscope.

"I shall go there at once. Please give me the address."

"But they're closed! They willnae open!" He had obviously not dealt with Mother before. He tried to pull the stethoscope away but it would not budge from her grip. After he reluctantly gave her the address, she released the stethoscope. The doctor plodded away, grumbling about persistent and irritating women.

"What are you doing?" asked Ian, his irritation barely suppressed.

"You want a motive. I will get you one!"

"You are fearsome stubborn, lady."

"Thank you, but compliments, while appreciated, are hardly necessary."

Ian almost smiled at that. A heavy pelting of rain on the window drew Mother's awareness to the fierce weather. "I suggest we borrow an umbrella." She picked up his notebook from the table and handed it to him. "To keep your theories from drowning."

CHAPTER TWENTY-FOUR

London, The Admiralty

Mycroft Holmes was addressing the same assembly of naval brass and high civilian personages who had attended the previous meeting.

Ramsgate only half-listened as Mycroft reviewed the latest strains in the smouldering relationship between Britain and Germany. Ever since the young Kaiser Wilhelm had dismissed the "Iron Chancellor" Bismarck (and his careful policy of balancing European power), relations between the two nations had deteriorated. As long as Germany concentrated her military might on her efficient army, Britain could continue her policy of remaining aloof from the European rivalries. But now the German Navy was led by Grand Admiral Tirpitz, who, by gaining the Kaiser's ear and shrewd moves in the Reichstag, was building a fleet in a direct challenge to the Royal Navy. Britain had to respond. She had a worldwide empire and a vast merchant fleet to protect. What's more, Britain was an island that could not feed her people. Necessities came by sea.

Kipling's poem, "The Big Steamers," drove home this point. It ended with the verse:

For the bread that you eat and the biscuits you nibble
The sweets that you suck and the joints that you carve

They are brought to you daily by all us Big Steamers—
And if any one hinders our coming you'll starve!

Kipling had done no more than give poetry to a hard reality. An imperial island nation could not survive without control of the sea. Britain had responded with a naval building programme of her own, and had also been forced into European alliances. The *Dreadnought* was merely Britain's latest response in a game of move and counter-move. Any sane person, on a moment's reflection, could see that the contest was pointless. Europe had never been more secure or prosperous. There was really nothing for the great powers to fight about. While Germany was late in the empire game and her hodge-podge of colonies made a very poor showing against the extensive holdings of the United Kingdom, Germany was quite wealthy without an extensive empire. Perhaps the young Kaiser simply wanted a big navy because his cousin on the British throne had one.

There was an old story that the architect who had been commissioned to design the Admiralty had brought their Lordships the plans for an insane asylum by mistake. Not wanting to admit the error, he presented the plans and they were approved. Ramsgate thought there was a certain irony in hearing the condition of a mad world in a building designed for lunatics. But then, it was also perhaps the first office building built by the British government, ushering in the modern era of an ever-expanding professional bureaucracy.

Mycroft finished up.

"… and if you get hopping immediately, you'll just make the train to Glasgow. I'll see you all tomorrow on board *Dreadnought*. Good luck."

The meeting broke up and most left at once. As Ramsgate hurried past, Mycroft halted him with a raised finger. "Any communication from Lady Dorrington?"

"Not a word. She's silent as a tomb."

CHAPTER TWENTY-FIVE

Millport Village

ightning illuminated the brass nameplate that read:

Millport Historical Society
By appointment only
10:00–2:00

Ian and Tasha, huddled under his umbrella, rushed through the fierce rain to the front door. Ian had offered her the sole use of the umbrella, but Mother insisted that they share. Ian complained that they should have waited for Constable Blake to return.

"You left word where to find us. It's more important to get you your evidence." Tasha pulled on the doorbell. There was a deep reverberation, like the peeling of Big Ben.

"Good God!" said Ian in surprise.

"It *is* rather loud," agreed Tasha. "Whoever is inside must be ..." She had a sudden realisation. "Deaf!"

A peephole in the door slid away, revealing the old doctor. "We're nae open!" he announced, and then slid the peephole shut. Tasha rose to the challenge and pulled madly on the bell wire. The cacophony was appalling.

"What are you doing?" shouted Ian over the din.

"I intend to get us in there!" said Tasha with finality.

"A quid says you don't!"

Ian's money was still on a table as lightning flashed outside the Historical Society's tiny reading room window. He paused from cleaning the two revolvers before him as he ruefully noted his money. More thunder and lightning drew his notice to the worsening of the storm.

"It's darn mean out there," noted Ian.

Tasha, half-hidden by stacks of ancient volumes, was too absorbed by her reading to notice the inclement weather. She simply continued her intense studies, placing one musty volume on a tall stack to her left—which represented several hours worth of her research—while reaching for another on an even larger pile of books on her right—the ones she had still yet to peruse. There were also two massive antique books, open and placed off on the corner.

Ian picked up Tasha's Webley British Bulldog Revolver, a dainty piece compared to his formidable and longer-barreled Colt six-gun. Its compact design, which could easily fit in a pocket, made the Bulldog the popular choice with plainclothes detectives, but its short barrel, made for close work, was not a marvel of long range accuracy. "I swear, Tasha, I could spit more on-target than this little Webley hog-leg of yours!"

There was again no response. He continued to clean the revolvers. Tasha intently studied a massive tome, running her finger along the page, tapping her digit excitedly. "Aha! Capital! Rewards to the persistent. As my famous colleague once exclaimed, 'if the green-grocer had such a thing as a laurel wreath, I should send for one!'"

Ian gave her his full attention. She laughed elatedly, read and explained: "The cult that flourished here in the seventh century, though they were occasionally misidentified as Druid ..."

"Weren't the Druids ancient Celtic priests or something?"

"Priests, wise men, physicians, mathematicians. Imagine Merlin from the Arthurian tales. But our group was more akin to demon worshippers. It's not conclusive, but they may have even practised some form of human sacrifice."

Ian motioned for her to continue. Tasha slid over one of the open books on the table's corner and pointed to a passage. "It seems that over time, animals replaced the human victims. The cult's symbol was ... the crescent-moon ... wonderful ... and they were called the Circle of the Smiling Dead!"

Ian leaned in.

"It gets better," she said with rising pleasure, and returned to the book in front of her. "The cult was led by a priestess who always assumed the ancestral name 'Deirdre.'"

"The name the girl screamed before she died, ain't it?"

Tasha nodded and then continued reading, "... they hated the ancient Christians and vowed to die rather than convert. They hid deep in the belly of the earth, and remained hidden until ... until one of their own betrayed them to the church for nine pieces of silver. And the name of this latter-day Judas was McGloury!"

CHAPTER TWENTY-SIX

The Caverns, Prison Chamber

I'm distressed you haven't been comfortable, Mr. McGloury," said Deirdre to a barrel-chested man in a nautical pea-coat, bound in chains to the ragged rock walls of a cramped chamber used as a prison cell. An oil lamp, sitting on the floor against the opposite wall, cast huge, lurid shadows throughout the craggy chamber. Deirdre watched from the entrance as a guard, in farmer's garb, roughly pulled off one of the prisoner's boots. "I'd have paid a visit sooner, but I've been so busy." Deirdre continued in cheerful conversation. "Still, as the first McGloury in over three hundred years to come home to Millport, well, I simply had to make time for you."

He tried to reach for her, fighting the short chains, but they constrained him well out of reach. "You scurvy little gutter-snipe!" he growled in a voice that was used to being in authority. The guard backhanded him with his own boot. McGloury's head—for this was the *real* McGloury and not the dissembling soft-handed imposter who had hired Tasha—snapped against the wall, and his anger changed to dread.

"Why ... why are you doing this?" The terror became more pronounced as he realised he was dealing with a madwoman.

"How quickly they forget. Your fate was decided the day you returned to Millport!" Her eyes took on a faraway look and her voice became a whisper. "No … it was decided long, long before that."

McGloury simply stared at her, vainly trying to make some sense of her words.

"I will exact the full penalty long after you are gone," continued Deirdre, still lost in the vision her mind was conjuring, "A retribution that will be forever!" Her mood altered, as if a switch had been turned and Deidre's passionate reverie ceased, her features again became impassive. She extended her hand and the guard obediently gave her McGloury's boot. "I need this for a little while, Mr. McGloury, but it will be returned before you leave us."

Not far away, in another equally small chamber, Von Traeger was lashing Boab, the bogus McGloury's "lost" collie, with a whip. Boab, beaten into mindless ferocity, snarled at the German, straining at his leash—which was tied to the wall—as Von Traeger took McGloury's boot from Deirdre and rubbed it in the animal's face. "He will be vicious at this scent, Geistliche Deirdre."

She snapped her fingers and Von Traeger stood away from the dog. Boab strained at the leash in feral desperation, as Deirdre, just out of reach, smiled faintly at his viciousness. She walked out, giving Von Traeger a rare nod of approval. "You have a way with animals." Von Traeger clicked his heels and jolted to attention with pride and Prussian precision.

CHAPTER TWENTY-SEVEN

Millport Village

Mother, still researching in the Historical Society reading room, was explaining her findings to Ian, "… and the Christians burned the Priestess Deirdre at the stake as a bana-bhuidseach—a witch. She vowed revenge on the McGloury clan, and revenge on all Christians—until the end of forever."

Tasha was quite pleased with herself. Ian couldn't deny the connections, but he was irked to admit it, "A thousand years is a powerful long time to hold a grudge."

"The old wheel turns slowly, Inspector, but the same spoke will come up again," she answered. "Three hundred years ago, practically yesterday, there was a resurgence of the cult—around the time of the Restoration. Priests were killed; churches in the area were destroyed. By coincidence, at that time, a McGloury was living on the croft, the first in memory to do so. He was murdered, found with the old '*Risus sardonicus* …'" She grinned ear-to-ear and Ian nodded in understanding. She added, "The signature of the Circle of the Smiling Dead."

Lightning flashed outside as the storm worsened, taking Ian's attention to the window. The distraction was short, and he watched Tasha out of the corner of his eye. He was impressed—and not at the storm. "It riles me to say so, but ma'am, you've struck pay-dirt."

Tasha raised her finger and gestured to the open books that littered the table. There was more. "That McGloury was warned of his death for three nights of three weeks. Nine nights. One for each piece of silver paid to his ancestor by the Christians." She stopped suddenly. "The ninth night!"

The realisation hit Mother like a fire-bell. She bolted from her chair, snatched up her Webley revolver from the table, as well as the one-pound note she had won in the bet, and raced out. Ian was lost for a second, then grabbed his heavy Colt revolver, and dashed after her.

CHAPTER TWENTY-EIGHT

McGloury Croft

Before Ian could halt the gig, Tasha—like Ian, soaking wet from the cold rain—leapt to the road, peering ahead to the ruins. Above the rain and fierce wind, they could hear the eerie chanting of more than a dozen voices.

"Utter fool that I was to desert him!" yelled Tasha over the din. "Look!"

The ruins odd appearance was even more distorted by the ferocity of the storm. The ancient shrine was torch-lit and full of black-robed people standing on various levels of the rocks. There were eighteen in all: nine men and nine women; every one of them wore masks that mimicked a goat's heads with exaggerated horns. The torches were sheltered from the elements by alcoves cut into the dolmens. They created a harsh contrast of flickering red light and dancing black shadows that that exaggerated the malevolent atmosphere. Some sort of ceremony was transpiring, and the gathered all gave voice to a rhythmic chant. The horns of the masks turned in unison to the altar stone, where there was erected a black-robed effigy of an ancient demon-god, with crescent-moons on the robe and flaring horns protruding from the distorted goat-like animal skull that formed the sinister head.

From the roadway, Tasha and Ian scrutinized the proceedings in front of them.

"I don't see McGloury!" yelled Ian.

"They have him. Depend on it!" said Tasha bitterly, as she drew her revolver and dashed to the ruins as fleetly as the mud-soaked ground would permit. Ian followed close behind.

Two masked men dragged a live goat to the altar. The robes of the effigy parted as Deirdre, in her priestess robes and bearing an ornate mask, emerged in flowing white with a crescent moon dangling near her breast. She raised a crude stone dagger and with one accurate stroke, slit the animal's throat left to right. The chanting abruptly stopped and, save for the rain—the wind had died down—there was silence. Deirdre addressed the assembly in a disguised whisper. She pointed to a dolmen and motioned, "Come here."

Tasha and Ian stepped from behind the towering monolith, weapons in hand. There they were, Mother and Ian, alone in these sinister ruins, surrounded by this silent, motionless mob of masked demon worshipers.

Deirdre, with a bend of her finger, bid them forward.

Tasha boldly marched in, but Ian, his eyes darting from place to place, followed nervously. They reached the altar, and he pointed his revolver at Deirdre. "Up with your hands ... ma'am."

He was ignored, even by Tasha. She was focused on Deirdre—who, with her face concealed and her voice disguised, Mother failed to recognise from their meeting at the Hermes. But she had put enough together to ask, "Deirdre, is it not?"

The priestess nodded.

Tasha nodded in return. "We meet at last."

Deirdre's smirk was just visible under the lower part of the mask. The cult members burst into laughter. Ian scowled at the masked faces made hideous by the malicious hysterics that surrounded them, but Mother kept her eyes on Deirdre. The priestess raised her finger and the laughter stopped. An impressive display of discipline.

"We've met before," came the mocking reply from behind the priestess's mask.

"When?" There was no answer. "Where is McGloury?" Again no answer, just Deirdre's maddening half-smile behind the ornate mask. "You are already responsible for two murders," continued Mother.

"Three," Deirdre whispered. "Now four." She dramatically raised her arm and at once there was a vicious howling and human scream from the direction of the cliff. Tasha spun to see, indistinct through the storm and distance, the blur of a dog lunging for the throat of the vague shape of a man. That shape screamed again.

"McGloury!" yelled Tasha as she sprang into action.

She heard Deirdre's mock sympathetic taunt. "Help him. You never fail."

As Tasha and Ian raced toward the cliff, Deirdre, unmoving and regal, removed her mask, revealing her luminous eyes. Somewhere, faint in her throat, was a chuckle. "The cleverest woman in Europe."

At that moment the "cleverest woman" was aiming her gun at the dog, but hound and human were intertwined as they struggled toward the cliff, making a clean shot impossible. She was too late.

The battle ended as man and beast tumbled over the precipice, their screams and howls vanishing with them. Mother stopped and staggered as if she'd been physically hit. Her mind screamed in protest. There was no point in giving it actual voice, and she bolted toward the cliff. She didn't hear Ian's warning—and would have ignored it if she had. Then the muddy ground crumbled under her feet and she slipped over the edge. She plummeted only for a second—Ian grasped her arm and, painfully, pulled her back up.

Mother's normal reserve was gone; she was desperate and fighting back tears. She had failed. Her client was dead.

After Ian pulled her over the edge, Tasha lay on the wet ground, rain pouring on her face. He stood and drew her to her feet. She silently walked past him and stared at the ruins. A flash of lightning illuminated them in vivid white light and black shadow. All was silent and deserted. Suppressing her rage, Tasha studied the now empty rocks, as Ian, behind her, spotted something at his feet.

He hurriedly retrieved a man's wallet while Tasha scrutinized the ruins. Ian slipped it into his coat pocket. Tasha turned to him, struggling for self-control. Her voice was strained. "McGloury's dog was missing this morning—and I didn't comprehend its importance." She stood stiffly, as if afraid to move. Ian placed his hands on her shoulders. She didn't react.

"Come on," he said softly.

Mother didn't move and answered through clenched teeth. "He came to me for protection!" She jerked away from the Inspector.

"Tasha!" Ian took her in his arms and turned her toward him while peering deep into her quivering face. He saw no longer the self-assured sleuth, but a beautiful and vulnerable woman. He kissed her and she responded, her arms circling his neck.

This intimate moment was not theirs alone.

CHAPTER TWENTY-NINE

The Caverns, Deirdre's Chamber

Deirdre, expressionless, watched Tasha and Ian with her *camera obscura*. Sebastian, in his naval commander's uniform, frowned down at Tasha's image. "Why don't you simply kill her?" he asked evenly. He expected a sharp retort, but to his surprise, Deirdre chuckled quietly, though she did not look away from the image on her viewing stone.

"Sebastian! You're jealous. How touching. Understand. If you kill someone they're dead. But to shatter the will, erode the spirit, destroy someone utterly ... that really does take a woman's touch. So understand that I ..."

She stopped as her concentration locked on the image of Ian leading Tasha into the cottage.

Sebastian walked over to the four-poster bed and parted the curtains. There I was, huddled in the corner of the bed. Something in the food they gave me had knocked me out. The effect of the drug on my seven-year-old body must have been severe.

I had been lured away from Nanny Roberts by a small puppy, reputedly sent as a gift from my Mother through Inspector Ramsgate, in the same park where the Admiralty officer had been murdered. My abduction was neatly done. The arrangements that brought us to the park seemed authentic. The note was on

Ramsgate's official stationary and said, "Look for a surprise." A Scottish Terrier puppy toddled up with a bright scarlet ribbon around its neck and a card attached. Nanny Roberts read the note, which said, "Follow me."

She set the adorable little creature on the ground, and it scuttled around the curve of the hedge. I was in hot pursuit, clutching my Teddy Bear tightly. Nanny Roberts kept to her bench and stayed with her reading, watching me as I ran. Nothing seemed amiss.

I followed the puppy, darting through the crack in the hedge. Someone's arms reached around me from behind. I have no idea if it was chloroform or some other substance, but I was out in seconds. My limp form was placed in a hidden compartment in a large double perambulator, and I was wheeled away, I suspect right past Nanny Roberts. Not enough time had passed to alarm her. I don't even know if it was Deirdre who kidnapped me or some other confederate.

After a full two minutes had passed, Nanny Roberts, now concerned, followed my path. She entered the hedge, but by then there was no one there—only my Teddy Bear, propped against the hedge with its black little eyes and sewn-on smile directed at Nanny. Then the puppy scampered up to her. There was another note tied to the scarlet ribbon, this one addressed to Lady Natasha Dorrington. Nanny Roberts scooped up the puppy and note, and ran to find the nearest constable.

Although I assume there were periods when I was awake, all I can recall with clarity was nodding off in that plush room behind the opium den in Limehouse ... a dreamlike image of a private train compartment ... and waking up on a fishing-smack in the Firth of Clyde. The hold of the small boat was dark, cold, and damp. The smell of the sea told me I was far from home and safety. I was terrified, and as events were to prove, with very good reason.

CHAPTER THIRTY

The McGloury Croft

Mother stared at the telegram. Her usually sharp mind was momentarily drained of all but the information tersely written in the old semaphore woman's precise handwriting on the rain-spattered telegraph form. It had been waiting inside the cottage, left by messenger earlier in the afternoon.

The lightning threw Mother into vivid relief. Ian, seeing Tasha stunned and staring blankly at the telegram, pulled it gently from her hands. Before he could read it, Mother said quietly, "My daughter—kidnapped! I must return to London!"

She turned and rushed to the door, but Ian grabbed her arm firmly.

"Not in this storm. The ferry can't get across."

"I must go!"

He pulled her to him. She pushed back, breaking his grip, shoved him away, and turned back to the door. Ian again clutched her arm. "Trying to get across now's a ticket to boot hill! You'll drown. Will that help your kid?"

Mother glowered at him in turmoil. She knew that leaving Millport Island was a physical impossibility, yet she also knew that I was in danger, and her impotence to act was tearing her apart. She buried her head in his chest and he stroked her hair. Her features distorted as her mind fought to regain control. There were no tears.

"In the morning, Tasha," he whispered.

CHAPTER THIRTY-ONE

The Caverns, Deirdre's Chamber

Deirdre ceaselessly watched on her *camera obscura*, as if staring at the image long enough could enable her vision to penetrate the walls to peer inside. Behind her, Sebastian was closing the curtains on the big four-poster bed.

"She's asleep. How much of your potions can a child endure?" he challenged.

Deirdre was annoyed at having to shift her attention away from the projection of the cottage. "Shouldn't you be back aboard *Dreadnought*?"

Her inflection nipped at his belligerence. "No, not until eight bells, four this morning ... or when the storm clears."

"You look tired. Go to sleep," she said, her contemplation again pinned to the cottage. He moved to her, but she ignored him and continued her expectant vigil.

Sebastian made one more attempt to engage her. "You've been right about everything. Half the government will be on board. We'll be at war with Germany in a week and then all of Europe will explode. Precisely as you planned it."

His praise had no effect. She kept staring, expressionless, into her device. Suddenly, in the reflection, the cottage light dimmed.

Deirdre leaned in closer, her fingers gripping the side of the viewing stone in anticipation. "Ah, Lady Dorrington, I predict you so very well."

Sebastian, hurt, impulsively pulled the lever cutting off the light from above and the image vanished. "And one more piece drops into place! Why this piece? Why her?"

Deirdre straightened and perceived Sebastian with surprised amusement. "You presume to question me."

His temper was up as he glared at her and warned, "You're risking a lot for a wee bit of pride. Kill her."

CHAPTER THIRTY-TWO

The McGloury Croft

Tasha and Ian were stretched out on a sheepskin before the fire, having just finished making love. Mother would later tell herself that the act was simply a mechanism to purge her frustrations, suppress her emotions, and allow her intellect to regain control. Then all her formidable powers—unhindered and sharp—would be singularly devoted to my rescue. And while her strategy would likely work, at that moment her eyes glistened with tears. Ian caressed her wet cheek.

"Human at last. I wasn't sure. You were like some kind of thinkin' machine."

She said nothing, for it was not the time for words, only physical release. Tasha drew closer and kissed him passionately.

Later, when only a few embers remained of the spent fire, the storm had abated, and all was at last quiet. Ian slept under the sheepskin, but Tasha was not beside him. She stood at the door, wrapped in a blanket. Ian's coat hung on a hook and she was searching through the pockets. She withdrew the wallet Ian had stealthily recovered at the cliff. Mother opened it and scanned the contents. She removed a folded document and read it by the dim oil lamp at the table.

She held a Mariner's Masters Certificate issued to Cedric McGloury in 1897.

Tasha's face lost its tender vulnerability and hardened. She sat at the table, set the document down, stretched out her long legs, and tented her palms and fingers. And there she sat, physically still; her mind moving pieces of a thought puzzle this way and that.

It was still dark as Ian opened his eyes to see Tasha, now in her cat-burglar attire, and holding an oil-lamp, bending close to him to stir him awake. "Ian. The storm's over—get dressed. Quickly."

"The storm …" he said groggily, then as awareness grew, "Oh, the ferry … I'm up."

Tasha picked up his trousers, draped over the back of a chair, and tossed them to Ian, who (remember, this was 1906) had moved behind a dressing screen. She then collected his shirt and tossed that over the screen as well.

"Here's your shirt. Would you mind a little last minute advice?"

"I reckon I surely wouldn't," he answered from behind the screen as he called for his vest (and he used the American term, instead of waistcoat). "And don't fret—you just high-tail it back to London and save that kid."

Tasha picked up the vest. "Oh, I think I'll be able to save her." She tossed the garment over the dressing screen. "By the by, that ruined church on the mainland, the one with the telescope trained on the *Dreadnought* ... if you're quick enough you may be in time, Inspector. Here's your tie."

He stepped out from behind the screen, nearly dressed, and caught the tie. "Be in time? In time for what?"

"To stop the Circle of the Smiling Dead from attacking the *Dreadnought*, blaming Germany, and provoking a major war. Their long brewing revenge on Christian Europe. I think the coat comes next." She flung it to him.

He stared at her and finally said, "Seems we've strayed a mite from your friend McGloury's murder—not to mention your daughter's kidnapping."

"While the man who was murdered last night was certainly McGloury, he was not the man who hired me. The man I knew was an imposter, used as bait to lure me to Millport Island, just as my daughter's abduction is a ruse to force my return to London."

Ian slipped on his coat and froze, eyeing her suspiciously.

"The genuine McGloury had served at sea," Mother explained pleasantly. "My imposter had not. There were no calluses on his hands, his walk was not the rolling stride of someone used to a life on ships. But the details hardly matter, Inspector." Her voice took on an icy tone. "Is it Inspector? Or perhaps your credentials are as assumed as your affection." She reached into her belt and withdrew the Mariner's Master Certificate.

Ian's tone hardened, "You've been just stringin' me along from the first!"

There was no emotion in Tasha's voice, "This is a very complex game and you've done rather well for a pawn." She threw him his hat and said coldly, "But now that you're dressed, let's visit the queen."

Ian drew his revolver from his pocket and aimed it at Mother. "I'm amazed you forgot this."

"I didn't. It isn't needed. Shall we go? We mustn't keep Deirdre waiting."

"I wish to heaven you'd returned to London!" he spat out through clenched teeth.

Mother noted his heightened passion, what it might portend and how it might be useful.

As Ian and Mother approached the altar stone, it sank into the mud and slid away uncovering a shaft with handholds hewn into the rock.

"As I suspected," said Tasha. "We are observed—and expected."

Grimly, Ian motioned for her to descend, following close behind. They vanished into the dark shaft, and the altar stone slid back into place. The ruins were again deserted, alone and gaunt against the night sky, leaving no visible evidence anyone had been there at all.

Chapter Thirty-three

The Caverns

The shaft emptied into a mammoth crypt. Tasha nimbly dropped to the floor and glanced around as Ian descended more slowly. He had to pocket his gun as he came down, clutching the foot- and hand-holds cleft into the stone shaft. He paused, still grasping the last hand-hold, and out came the revolver, keeping Mother covered, as he dropped to the ground.

Mother regarded him disdainfully, "I have mentioned how superfluous that six-gun is."

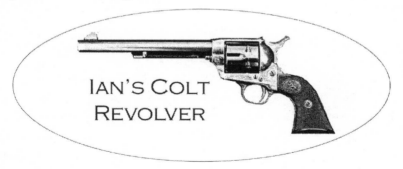

IAN'S COLT
REVOLVER

Ian hesitated, his Colt wavering, then returned to cover Mother. He motioned for her to walk ahead, deeper into the chamber.

Ancient skeletal remains festered in wall alcoves and under shrouds on stone slabs. More tortured faces were carved all around and everything was layered in generations of dust and webbing. Ian guided Tasha through the under-world maze, as her eyes ceaselessly inspected everything. She ran her finger through the powdery filth. "A pre-Roman Golgotha. Last dusted around the time of William the Conqueror."

Ian led her to a huge visage, mouth agape, carved on the far wall. Tasha stopped before it and asked Ian, "This Deirdre has gone to singular effort to humiliate me. Why?"

"You'll get your answers in here." He put his hand on the control lever, but didn't depress it. Some of his anger faded. He whispered, "I'm sorry it came to this."

Mother, her neutral expression unchanged, nodded. It was answer enough. Ian's anger had been directed against himself. He depressed the lever and the ancient wooden jaw slid away exposing a passage. Without waiting for a signal, Tasha entered.

She stepped into a lofty tunnel, like a large mine shaft. Many entrances were visible. Some were crude tunnels that simply appeared in the walls. The bigger shafts were like the eye sockets of skulls. Others had demonic carvings, mostly more faces, with the open portals giving the impression of screaming mouths hewn into the stone, creating a passageway of pain and rage. Torches were set at intervals and also an occasional oil lamp mixing yellow light with the flickering of crimson open flames. The stone arches above the torches were stained black with soot. Wooden shipping crates were stacked irregularly and there were tiers of cable spooled and stored in depressions along the walls. Ian, his gun still trained on Tasha, entered behind her.

She cocked her head at the supplies. "Now here's a well-stocked little pantry no private army should be without."

Suddenly, a voice with a thick Scot accent boomed at them from ahead. "Staun where ye are!" Out from the tunnel shadows hobbled a crusty old sweeper man, holding a dust-pan and sweeping broom. "Clean yer boots!" he ordered as he tossed Tasha a well-used rag.

She wiped the thick mud from her feet. "There are some things that surprise even me." She tossed Ian the rag. "Like these crates. British ammunition, German machinery ... No playing favourites here. And these ..." She walked over to a stack of crates, each with markings in a different language. "English. German. French. Russian."

"Deirdre's message ... to incite the soldiers to mutiny after the war starts," Ian confirmed Tasha's assertion.

"It would have to exceedingly convincing," said Mother with asperity.

"Back in America—around 1776—a lot of folks were on the fence about the revolution. They knew things were bad, but didn't know what to do. A man named Thomas Paine wrote something called 'Common Sense.' People read it—and a whole lot of them got off that fence and picked up guns."

"But that was Thomas Paine," replied Mother.

"Deirdre's that good. I read it—she almost made a believer out of me," said Ian as he tossed back the rag to the sweeper. "Almost."

The four midgets from the Admiralty murder, dressed in German sailor suits, walked into the tunnel. One carried a sextant and nautical chart. They filed past and vanished into a passage.

Tasha discerned them with dispassionate interest. "MacMurdo's Leprechauns, no doubt. Shall we continue the tour?"

They stepped onto a wide stone platform overlooking the main chamber. It was an immense cavern whose roof and sides faded into the darkness. The fierce carvings were sparser but more massive. The screaming granite face behind them was so large that its open mouth both framed and dwarfed the big tunnel through which they had entered. The huge eye sockets gleamed red as deeply recessed crystals reflected the flickering torches. The colossal space was very dim, mostly lit by spotty torches, but here and there were brighter pods of light, cast by oil lamps.

The largest of these illuminated pools was on a makeshift pier at the edge of a lagoon that seemed to have no end as its true expanse melted into the murky blackness of the cavern. The carvings died away as the grotto extended into the water leaving the natural cave unembellished. On the pier stood construction equipment and many crates. This was obviously the scene of much activity. Tied alongside the wharf was a small coastal submarine with a huge conning tower, far larger in disproportion to the size of the ship. Mother, who kept up with current events, recognised the conning tower as a perfect replica of a German Fleet U-boat, right down to the Imperial German Navy marking. Tasha easily surmised that the lagoon opened to the firth. There were twenty men, mostly in two groups and dressed in no distinguishing way. The larger group was engaged in some activity around the U-boat, making it ready for sea. The other group, of just five men, was eating a supper of mutton and bread at a wooden table.

Tasha turned her head to Ian, standing grimly behind her. She was impressed. "There is genius behind this. Where is she?"

The hatch of the conning tower opened, and Von Traeger emerged, spotting them on the platform above. *"Willkommen!"* he shouted. The other men shifted their attention to the platform and grinned at the sight of Mother as a prisoner. A few applauded, but Ian angrily cut them short. "Where's Deirdre?"

Von Traeger pointed down the grotto. "On the mainland. She will return soon."

Ian bound Tasha to the wall in the same prison chamber, using the same chains, that earlier held the genuine McGloury. Though her features betrayed no emotion, he avoided meeting her eyes as he clamped her in irons.

Then, after he had left Mother alone for over an hour, he reentered the chamber with his revolver ready. "I've brought you some vittles. I'm going to let you loose so you can eat."

Another man entered with a tray of food. As he walked into the torch light Tasha could see the bulky form of Constable Blake.

"Is this entire island working for Deirdre?" she asked as Blake set down the tray.

"Most of it, ma'am," said Blake.

"Including, I fear, the woman at the telegraph station?" Ian nodded.

"Of course, in that case the telegram regarding Laura's abduction might be a canard."

Blake shook his head, "No ma'am. That was real."

"Indeed! We shall see about that! However, I am accurate in assuming my message to London was never sent—at least not in the form I intended."

"As the Americans say, ma'am, the cavalry won't be coming to your rescue," replied Blake with unexpected humour.

"That'll do, Blake," snapped Ian as he undid Mother's manacles. The chains were too short to allow enough movement for eating. Tasha rubbed her wrists and gratefully attacked the meal that Blake had placed on a small, sturdy wooden table. There was nothing "lady-like" about her appetite—she even ate from the end of the spoon instead of more properly from the side. She had no fear that the food was poisoned, for Deirdre conspicuously wanted her alive for reasons that could only be unpleasant.

"It's only mutton pie, I'm afraid," said Blake.

"By way of the cliff on McGloury's croft," she alleged between bites. "Must be a lot of mouths to feed down here. I take it those nautical midgets were employed on occasion to assist getting the sheep into this cavern." Tasha paused in her eating and gave Ian a nod. "Still. Thank you."

"We ain't cruel, Tasha."

"Ah. One hungry woman upsets you, but the impending death of millions somehow fails to prick your delicate conscience." She handed the now empty bowl back to Blake.

There was no response. Ian, grim and taciturn, just watched her.

Later, Ian, Blake, and Von Traeger stood on the pier as Sebastian and the man who posed as McGloury, as I will continue to call him, expertly shipped oars and moored Deirdre's rowboat.

She hurriedly disembarked from the stern—Deirdre disliked travelling over water—and Von Traeger noisily clicked his heels to attention. She glided past him to Ian, her keen eyes asking an unspoken question. He frowned and shook his head "no."

Deirdre held an oil lamp close to Tasha's face. Tasha was bound again to the walls of the prison chamber. Each studied the other; Deirdre had assumed her veneer of impenetrability. Tasha regarded her adversary with a touch of boredom, sighing, "Wasn't our last game enough for you?"

Deirdre drew away and in a quiet voice, commanded, "Let her loose."

Sebastian and Ian were there. Ian, scowling, slipped the key from his pocket and unshackled Tasha. Deirdre handed Sebastian the lamp, walked to Tasha and appraised her, studying every womanly curve.

Sebastian's frown deepened as he barely controlled his rage at this dangerous charade. Ian shifted uneasily from foot to foot.

Deirdre grazed Tasha's neck with one hand then slid it down her shoulder toward her breasts. Ian was livid, but Tasha grinned as if nothing untoward were happening. Then she explosively backhanded Deirdre and spun away. As she completed her spin, Tasha pulled out her dainty Webley revolver from a hidden pocket. "I'm amazed you forgot this, Ian."

WEBLEY
"BRITISH BULLDOG"

Deirdre, maliciously calm, picked herself up from the ground. "Then Ian must take it back."

He didn't move until Deirdre turned her stern, compelling eyes on him. He walked to Tasha, but Mother firmly held her ground. "Ian ... I will use this." Mother would certainly kill if there were no other choice, but something was ringing alarm bells in her brain. Ian met her eyes, ignoring the maw of her revolver. Tasha made her decision and pressed the trigger. Nothing happened, and that's what she expected. She gave a cold smile and handed the Webley to Ian. Deirdre extended her hand, and he grudgingly handed it over.

"No firing pin," noted Deirdre. "How careless. Use your brilliant mind and not your heart, my dear. Is Ian the type to make so elementary a mistake?"

Ian glared at Deirdre. "Why don't you leave her be?"

Deirdre handed the Webley back to Ian and circled the chamber, eyeing Tasha, halting at the entrance. "Good thinking, Ian." She feigned a sad smile at Mother. "You don't like me, do you? I'll just have to find amusement elsewhere."

She snapped her fingers and McGloury shoved me, gagged and trembling, into the chamber. Mother instantly comprehended Deirdre's meaning. I can still see the raw terror on her face, which would haunt my dreams, appear in my waking moments, and hasn't faded in over seventy-five years. Mother tensed to spring into action, but the barest nod from Deirdre caused Ian to draw his revolver. I don't know what horrified me more—the deadly Colt, or seeing Mother incapacitated, her breath caught in her throat.

Deidre, void of passion, ordered Ian, "Aim at the child."

Ian didn't move, but his jaw clenched. Deidre, with a slight motion of her head, gave a silent order to McGloury. He reached for Ian's revolver. That snapped Ian to reality. He exhaled and glared, but did nothing as McGloury grasped the gun and placed the end of its barrel against my forehead. I shook with dread. Deidre returned her regard to Tasha.

"Bind her," Deirdre whispered to Ian.

Ian, fuming, forced Mother back to the wall and secured the chains. I tried to scream, but the gag was too tight. I wrenched free and ran to Mother. Deirdre stopped me. We strained to touch each other. Tears were streaming down my face. Every nightmare I'd ever dreamed had become a terrible reality. Deirdre's grip was like steel, and she shoved me back to McGloury, ordering breathlessly, "Take her to my chamber." McGloury lifted me by the waist with one hand. Ian brusquely retrieved his revolver, and McGloury, ignoring my frantic kicking, hauled me away. I was helpless—powerless to help myself or Mother—and I despised myself for it.

Mother was now desperate, stripped of all affectation and arrogance. Her impenetrable armour had been obliterated. In me, Deirdre had found the weapon to shatter it. "Don't, please. She's only a child."

Deirdre, her aware eyes gleaming, followed me, passing a frustrated Sebastian. She said to him caringly, "You had better get some sleep." He glowered and left.

Deirdre noticed Ian, also fuming. "You've been a disappointment to me, Ian." Then as if remembering something, she smiled warmly to Mother. "I told you we'd play again soon." Then in a soft whisper that still mocked, "Good night, Tasha."

Deidre glided down the tunnel, her soft footfalls receding. Ian cast his eyes to Tasha and she met his gaze. Her voice was quiet, but desperate. "Ian, you must stop her."

He picked up the lamp and staggered to the cell entrance. His fingers gripped the doorframe as if trying to crush the granite entrance to Tasha's prison.

Mother pleaded, "You can stop her. She's insane …"

He halted, keeping his back to her, torn apart by conflicting allegiances.

Mother, striving to reach the compassion she knew was within, entreated, "Laura is an innocent child. You can stop her! You *must* stop her! Please!"

He walked away. Mother screamed after him, "Ian!" She pulled furiously at her bonds. As strong as Mother was, the iron was stronger. She collapsed to the floor, waiting in horrible anticipation. Then, chords of a harp began and Tasha heard Deirdre's clear, lyrical voice, singing the old ballad (which to this day I cannot listen to) "Come Live with Me and Be My Love."

Deirdre, in her chamber, sat and sang serenely at her ornate harp, her delicate fingers floating across the strings. She sang, sitting erect, her priestess robe draped elegantly and pulled tight at the waist, her crescent-moon necklace reflecting the flickering lamplight. She was a queenly vision of calm. I've often thought how womanly at odds this was with her malignant nature.

I lay in her huge four-poster bed, watching in terror as McGloury, at the table, mixed a solution from little vials, and then poured the liquid into a hypodermic syringe. Deirdre followed my gaze and stopped singing. She regarded me through half-closed eyes, then resumed the haunting ballad.

I prayed for Mother to burst into that room and save me. I closed my eyes, hoping that when I opened them, she would be there. But when I opened my eyes, there was McGloury. He seized me and jabbed the needle into my arm. I bit my lip at the pain, but I was determined to be brave and did not scream.

Deirdre waved McGloury away. He set the syringe on the table and left. I started to shudder, as if my blood became ice. My eyes dilated and my head, which now seemed heavy as stone, sunk against the headboard.

Deirdre moved from her harp, but her superb voice maintained the song as she approached me. The final notes faded away. My eyes closed but I could feel her finger gliding lightly across my shoulder. I opened my eyes.

Deirdre was a blur, a vague form with an arm skimming back and forth across my shoulders. Then the image sharpened. Deirdre had become the demon-god carved into the roof of the chamber. In my hallucination, this horror was no longer stone, but alive with red-glowing eyes and blood-encrusted fangs. Upon its forehead a fiery crescent-moon spat scarlet flames. I know now what I saw wasn't real. Some part of me then must have known it wasn't real, but it didn't help. It didn't help either the little girl I was, or the young woman I grew to be. That beast from my mind would live with me, torturing me with my helplessness and poisoning me with buried anger that my Mother would permit this horror to happen to me. I saw Deirdre's hands become great, misshapen talons, rough and jagged, with sharp claws that ripped into my flesh. My eyes saw blood stain my white blouse in ever expanding, crescent-shaped pools.

Mother heard my screams. They mixed with my sobs as they distorted and echoed throughout the chambers and tunnels. Mother, in a frenzy, pulled against her bonds like a penned-up animal. The manacles held and it was she, not the chains, that shattered. She howled helplessly and sank to her knees, weeping.

Deirdre's fingers floated down my arm, and I screeched again, for I saw some sick, scaly nightmare prodding me, and at each touch, blood flowed from my skin. Then her hand moved to my face. Deirdre, in reality, must have just brushed my lips with her fingertips, but to me, my face was ripped away. My tiny hands clutched helplessly at the sheets, and as my reality became a vision of hell that no child should or could imagine, I shrieked until my throat was raw.

In the huge main chamber, Sebastian sat at the table, listening as my shrieks ate him up inside. My screeching echoed, and the men stopped their work. Von Traeger, at the submarine, attempted to divert himself by cleaning his monocle, but he noticed the hard expressions exchanged between Blake and McGloury, who stood on the dock.

Sebastian glared across the table at Ian, as thoroughly miserable as himself. The two men stared into each other's eyes. Ian grabbed his mug of ale and angrily tossed it against the stone wall, then stalked away up the stairs. Sebastian noted the Inspector's outburst suspiciously.

Mother was kneeling on the ground, staring at the rough stone floor, her mouth a hard line, her expression inscrutable. Ian, unseen by her, stood bitterly at the entrance. My screaming peaked and then abruptly stopped. In a moment, only naked silence filled the cavern.

The workers in the main chamber stood frozen. No one made a sound. Sebastian had left—the table was empty.

Sebastian was hidden in the shadows of the tunnel outside Mother's prison chamber, observing as Ian drew his revolver and entered. Having seen enough, Sebastian silently slipped away.

CHAPTER THIRTY-FOUR

The Caverns

Ian had been honest in telling Mother he was born on Millport. He loved the beauty of the island, but detested its grinding poverty. He migrated to America with his family in 1878 and, like many, went West to seek his fortune. Wealth eluded him, but he had a penchant for law enforcement and became a sheriff in Montana.

The feeling of freedom, that anything was possible in this new land, darkened as corruption tempted him. He soon found it profitable to look the other way when gambling halls cheated, and they were generous in their gratitude. Some of the ill-gotten money was sent to his elderly parents who had returned to Millport. Then two things changed: a citizen's committee exposed the corruption, and Ian was replaced by a new—and honest—sheriff. The timing was a blessing, for Ian received word that his parents were ailing and, using money he'd saved, returned to Millport to care for them. The trip home and medical bills soon exhausted his funds. Ian had to earn money, so he returned to his most gainful vocation: law enforcement.

He became an inspector for the City of Glasgow—the first modern police force in the world—and, at his request and though it was stretching the city boundaries, Millport Island became one of his responsibilities.

Ian was determined to be honest and paid adequately, but his salary wasn't enough to meet his parents' needs. He watched helplessly as one, and then the other, died. The sorrow—and bitterness—gave strength to the germ of corruption that had not been eradicated when he fled America. It waited only to infect again. And Deirdre, who discovered Ian's past and knew that having the local constabulary in her pocket would be useful, made it her business to recruit him.

Ian, like many, thought that war was inevitable. As long as conflict was coming, despite anything he could do, he had no problems making a profit. But that was as far as his corruption went. He had not wanted to think about how far Deirdre might go, or how personal her plan might become. Now he had to grapple with what he had done, and decide what he would do next.

Meanwhile, I was sprawled face down on the bed, sobbing into the pillow. Deirdre, though I couldn't see her, sat in front of a mirror, brushing her hair in manic calm. There was a knock at the entrance, and Sebastian anxiously entered. "Deirdre ..." he started, but she raised her hand.

"I know," she whispered.

Tasha glared at Ian as he unlocked the manacles on her left arm. He paused, noting her intensity. Mother slipped her left arm free while rattling the iron chains that constrained her other arm. Ian slipped the key into the lock, swallowed and said with regret, "There's a lot of things I've made myself live with ..."

Mother slid her right wrist free and stood up, her fury rising. Ian reached into his coat and grasped Mother's Webley revolver, "... and there's things I ..."

Tasha backhanded him. The Webley clattered to the floor. Mother, her eyes on Ian, stooped and retrieved it—the firing pin had been replaced—then aimed at Ian. Ian's knuckles wiped a trickle of blood from his mouth, "We need to go."

She lowered the gun, stepping past him in contempt. "Take me to Laura," she said, cold as death.

Mother and Ian were soon at the entrance to Deirdre's chamber. Mother signaled and they rushed in to find Deirdre at her table reviewing some charts. She coolly set them down and glanced at her visitors. Mother scanned the chamber. I was nowhere in sight. The bed was neatly made up.

"Where's Laura?" Mother intoned.

"We are very much alike, the two of us. Ask Ian," Deidre said.

Ian scowled at Deirdre. "You both think too much ... but she's got a heart."

Deirdre smiled softly and shook her head. "Your interest in her body wasn't the heart, Ian."

Mother could not have been less interested in any of this. "Where's Laura?" she demanded while aiming her revolver at Deirdre's head.

"Behind you," was her answer.

Mother felt the terror even before she turned back to the entrance. Sebastian, Von Traeger, and McGloury were there. I was limp and unconscious in the imposter's arms, and the German had the tip of his foil resting against my neck. Once more, because of me, Mother was powerless.

Deirdre removed the gun from Mother's hand. "It's still my move, Lady Dorrington. When you get emotionally involved, your wonderful mind rather dulls."

Mother did not answer, but her concentration fixed upon me. Deirdre noticed her anxious scrutiny.

"I will allow you this, your daughter was not harmed ... physically," said Deirdre.

"Whatever you did to her ..."

"... is forever. Her mind, her essence, will be filled by me." Deirdre turned to me, her hands travelling over—but not touching—my comatose body. "Let that be your dying thought, Lady Dorrington."

"What horror created this darkness inside? Did someone do this to you as a child? I pity the life that has filled you with such hate," replied Mother.

Deirdre snapped back to Tasha, her features darkened; but her flicker of anger was replaced by haughty mirth. "A scavenger of clues presumes to pity a Priestess." She shook her head. "That was hardly worthy of you. You must be wretchedly desperate."

Deirdre gracefully walked to Ian. "And Ian. What shall we do with you?" She lowered her head in mock sadness and turned back to Mother. "Concede the game?"

"You may fool the faithful with your 'prophecies, witches, and knells,'" mocked Mother, as she quoted satiric lyrics from W.S. Gilbert, "but in this 'game' you are merely a clumsy amateur."

Deirdre was surprised.

Mother knew that survival—hers, mine, perhaps millions more—depended on repressing her rage and taking her mind back under control. The hot rage cooled for the moment, she suppressed all emotion and forced total clarity. Mother continued, as if giving a lecture, "Permitting me to discover the real McGloury's Master Certificate ... shocking inattention to detail."

Deirdre cocked her head sternly at Ian. "It's so hard to get good help these days. Still, you've lost, Lady Dorrington."

Mother gave a little shrug. "We'll see."

"Why won't you admit it?" said Deirdre with quiet intensity. She moved closer, running her eyes over Mother. "What a waste. When we finish here, demolition charges will seal this cave forever."

"Won't you miss your little kingdom?"

"I'll soon have a much bigger one. This I bequeath to you. You'll be in here then."

"And Laura?"

"Can't you 'deduce' her fate? I'm going to bring her up for you. I will give her a glorious destiny. Your daughter will become me."

Tasha's face betrayed nothing.

But Deirdre knew Tasha's heart and could barely suppress her glee. She stepped seductively to Ian. "I'm going to forgive you, Ian." She embraced him. "I've a heart, too. Try and reach it."

She kissed him, her hands slid around his neck, her nails rubbed against his skin. They started to press. He knew all about the poison. He tried to push her away, but the finger-nails dug deeper. Any more movement would puncture the skin. "Hold me tighter, Ian," she taunted. The nails suddenly withdrew and she pushed him away. "No, you deserve a lingering death. One that gives you time to contemplate. You both do."

Moments later, Ian was tossed into the sacrificial chamber by McGloury and two other armed men who promised Ian they would be back soon. The door was slammed shut and Ian tried rushing the door—it was an instinct—though his intellect told him the stout wooden barrier wouldn't budge, and it did not.

To Sebastian's surprise, Deirdre was morosely watching me, passed out on her bed. He straightened out his immaculate naval uniform in the mirror and could see us in the reflection. "You didn't need to torture a child!"

Deirdre altered her notice—as if only just aware he was there at all—to him, and her dour mood lightened. "I have been neglecting you, Sebastian. And now you must leave for the most dangerous task of all, to be on board when the *Dreadnought* is attacked." She poured two snifters of brandy.

With all thoughts of me gone, Sebastian relished her rare moment of affection. "I'll be high on the bridge, far above the danger." He raised his glass for a toast. "We've come a long way together."

"Yes. And now we stand together on the precipice of a new age. My dear, Sebastian, you believe that my contest with Lady Dorrington is a personal matter. Can't you understand, it is a battle between her world and ours. You see who is in chains."

"And the child?" he asked.

"I was not being cruel. I was preparing her. I was honest with Lady Dorrington; under my guidance, the child is our future."

Deirdre handed Sebastian his snifter. "To the destruction of Christendom."

He shook his head. "To a remarkable woman."

Deirdre lowered her eyes in humble appreciation, but the diffidence was fleeting, and as she lifted her glass for the toast, those same eyes glinted in anticipation.

In the prison chamber, McGloury kept Mother covered as Von Traeger re-secured her chains.

Tasha baited the German with a haughty amusement. "I've always felt that your reputation with a rapier was in excess of your ability, Baron."

"You will not have the opportunity to find out, Fraülein," he answered as he checked her manacles.

"Life may surprise you. I'm sure a director of Germany's third-largest armaments empire never expected to keep the company of a madwoman in a Scottish cave." Mother's attention reverted to the chamber entrance. "For you are mad, Deirdre."

Deirdre was standing in the entrance, and silently ordered the two men away. They left the lantern and departed without a word. The two women were alone.

"You'll never win," Tasha started the conversation. "You hope the war will last for years and that millions of desperate men will rally to you. They will never come. They will reject you."

Deirdre moved closer, their eyes locked into each other. Deirdre was inscrutable, but Tasha detected a tension near the surface.

"Do your celebrated deductive skills include predicting the future?" Deirdre's words were mocking, but her voice trembled quietly.

Tasha made certain she sounded pleasantly detached, almost conversational. "I require no crystal ball to know that your vision sees only power, your cult offers only fear, and you are too blind to see that you cannot build a lasting world on that. It will crumble and be rejected, as you will be rejected. There is no cleverness that can prevent it. And somehow in me, you sense this truth." Deirdre, her expression unaltered, continued to study Mother, who continued, "You're a very frightened woman, Deirdre. So terrified that you had to come and see me in chains. Does it help?"

Deirdre became suddenly vehement. "I have your daughter. I have you. Tomorrow I'll start a war that will shatter Europe. I will destroy this stronghold of perversion that has ruled for a thousand years, and you can't lift a finger to stop me. You're beaten. Admit it!"

Mother shook her head.

"Admit it!" Deirdre repeated.

Tasha's only response was a patient smile and another slight shake of her head. Deirdre erupted, backhanding Tasha with all the strength she could command. The blow didn't remove Tasha's triumphant smile. Deirdre, shaken by her own emotions and loss of control, for the first time looked frightened. She composed herself, regaining her mask-like armour. "You'll admit it after tomorrow, Lady Dorrington. The world will admit it for you."

CHAPTER THIRTY-FIVE

The Ruined Church & *H.M.S. Dreadnought*

At first light, the ruined church overlooking Greenock Harbour and the *Dreadnought* were barely visible in the thick fog.

The "monk" squinted through his telescope and shrugged to another bogus monk standing behind him.

"Send the message, 'Target obscured in fog. Will report developments.'"

The monk wrote the message on a slip of rice paper and attached it to the leg of a pigeon. He leaned out the window and released the bird, sending it on its unerring way to Deirdre.

On the bridge of His Majesty's Ship, *Dreadnought*, Captain Summerlee observed the fog that swirled outside the scuttle. He sighed helplessly to Mycroft Holmes, who stood next to the Executive Officer (called "Number One" in the Royal Navy), just outside the hatch on the wing of the bridge, which was encased by fog. Nothing else was visible through the wheelhouse ports.

Summerlee stepped through the hatch, joining them in the damp mist, and took a sip of cocoa. "If you want the press-boat to spot us at sea, Mr. Holmes, we'll have to wait out the fog."

Sebastian, in letter-perfect uniform, entered through the hatch. "Their Lordships are complaining about the delay, sir."

Summerlee thanked Sebastian and then grinned to his Exec. "Try and soothe those exalted tempers, Number One. And send up that security chap." Summerlee was not delighted at having a ship full of Members of the House of Lords, Commons, and other high-ranking officials underfoot. They were acting as if the *Dreadnought* was their personal pleasure yacht, and his main duty was seeing to their comfort and answering endless, and often pointless, questions.

The Exec saluted. "Aye, aye, sir," and smartly went about his business.

CHAPTER THIRTY-SIX

The Caverns

In the large cavern, Deirdre was standing on the pier near the U-boat. She read the message sent by the pigeon and, unperturbed, crumpled it. Men were working all around her, some stringing cable to boxes of cordite across the lagoon near the sea entrance.

Outside the mouth of the cave, the fog was an impenetrable sheet of solid grey. Von Traeger emerged from the hatch in the conning tower and stared at the mist. "Your plan is useless in the nebel! They must identify the U-boat as German ..."

"The fog will not be a problem."

Von Traeger snorted. "Do you claim to control the weather, Priestess?"

"I do not let it control me. They will wait out the fog, Baron. As will we."

Mother was alone, still chained in the small rocky cell. She heard footsteps passing up and down the outside shaft, and indistinct voices. Though deducing from the increased activity that Deirdre's plan was hatching, for the moment, there was nothing Tasha could do but wait. She forced herself to accept that fact, and focused on what to do if the situation changed.

In the sacrificial chamber, Ian was suspended above the pit by a rope around his waist, secured with a pulley arrangement to the wall and ceiling. His wrists were also bound with thick knots and tied behind his back. McGloury lit a candle that protruded from the eye socket of a goat's skull, an inch below the rope, close enough to eventually sever it. "You must have left your common sense back on the prairie, cowboy. Did you really ken you'd get away with it, man?" McGloury inspected his handiwork while lecturing, "Deirdre's resurrected our old ways. She said this was the original purpose of this peculiar chamber." Then he added gleefully, "You're revivin' an old tradition."

"Glad to oblige," came Ian's polite, but edgy, reply.

McGloury snorted, "A pity you weren't so obliging in your loyalty to Deirdre."

"You don't have your smiling brand on me. It was just business."

McGloury gave a short laugh. "You see, Deirdre's got a bit of obsession about betrayal—you might recall the history of these caverns. Aye, betraying her was a daft thing to do, and very poor business." McGloury blew out the match, tossing it to the ground as he joined two armed men standing at the chamber entrance beside the sweeper man. The sweeper gave McGloury a withering look and swept up the match.

They all left, but McGloury leaned back in, "I suggest you use the time to contemplate the error of your ways." McGloury motioned his thumb at the rope, already beginning to singe from the candle, and added, "I'd do it with some haste," then left closing the door.

The sweeper man brushed some dirt into his dust-pan and emptied it into the pit.

Near the lagoon entrance, Deirdre's men finished wiring the crates of cordite.

Deirdre yelled across the water, "Put the detonator in the escape chamber!" The men waved in acknowledgement.

Von Traeger took note of the fog. "*Mein Priesterin!*" He barked in relief. "I think the fog is burning away."

Outside, the fog was thinning, and the grey sky took on a faint tinge of blue.

CHAPTER THIRTY-SEVEN

The Ruined Church & *H.M.S. Dreadnought*

he monk grinned in satisfaction as, through his telescope, the rapidly thinning mist unmasked the outline of the battleship below him in the firth.

Aboard the *Dreadnought*, Commander Bernard, appearing a little green around the gills, staggered to the bridge in a uniform altered more for a yachting regatta. He gave a weak salute to Captain Summerlee and leaned unsteadily against the bulkhead.

Ramsgate strolled in behind Bernard and nodded cheerfully to Sebastian and Summerlee. "I must say, breakfast was excellent. The navy always travels first class."

"Please ..." Bernard said faintly.

Summerlee stared at Bernard in amazement. "The man's sea sick! In port?"

"Naval Intelligence," offered Mycroft as an explanation.

Summerlee nodded in understanding then turned back to Bernard. "You may inform their Lordships that we're getting underway."

Bernard tried to carry on his end of the conversation (though all that was required was a perfunctory "Aye, aye, sir."). "Good. They've been as impatient as infants." Bernard took a step forward then retreated back to the bulkhead for support. He held up his hand, signaling he was fine and continued haltingly, "Lord Baskerville keeps demanding to know whose idea it was to put the crows-nest behind the smokestack."

"It's not a 'crow's-nest'!" protested Summerlee testily. "And it won't be a problem!"

High above the bridge, two ratings—as sailors are called in the Royal Navy—in the crow's-nest (really a spotting platform) stared down with concern at the smokestack below them. The oily black coal cloud was growing thicker, but, luckily, blowing away from them.

"Whose idea was it to put that there?" asked the first rating.

"I'd like to 'ave 'im up 'ere when we turn into the wind." contended his mate.

"Coo. Who'd sell a farm and go to sea?"

The conversation was cut short by a deep blast of the ship's whistle. The white steam from the whistle swirled around them.

On deck, levers were pulled, the capstan rotated, and the anchor chain emerged from the black waters of the firth, one huge studded link at a time. Sailors with hoses drenched the chain in a high-pressure stream, cleaning off all mud and sea-life as it slid through the hawsehole.

On the bridge, the telegraph indicator was rung down to "Ahead Slow."

Water boiled about the stern as the four gigantic screw propellers started their revolutions.

In the ruined church, the monk saw black smoke erupt from the *Dreadnought's* twin funnels and the battleship start to make way. With his eye still glued to the telescope, he excitedly ordered the second monk to send the message. Watching the battleship move majestically out of the anchorage, he found that he admired her ... she was a beautiful ship. Her business-like lines radiated power, efficiency and functional elegance.

Anyone who could read a newspaper knew that the *Dreadnought* had altered the balance of naval power. She would give her name to an entire class of ships and, the British government proclaimed, make old-style battleships as obsolete as wooden, sail-powered, ships of the line. That wasn't entirely accurate, but one fact stood out: naval power would now be estimated by the number of *Dreadnought*-style ships in the fleet. The great powers raced to complete as many *Dreadnought*-type ships as their will and national treasure allowed. Britain was ahead with one finished and three more soon to be laid down. Germany had none. First Sea Lord, Admiral Fisher, boasted, "We shall have ten Dreadnoughts at sea before a single foreign Dreadnought is launched!"

The *Dreadnought* was the darling of the naval world and, even more, the public. And because of that, the perfect tool for Deirdre's plan. The monk rubbed his hands with glee and grinned to his companion. "It's going to work, lad. We've waited centuries, and now the day has come. If only my grandfather and father were here, they'd dance a jig."

The other monk nodded in grinning agreement. "Aye, Deirdre's a wonder!"

CHAPTER THIRTY-EIGHT

The Caverns

Von Traeger, at a wooden table in the main chamber, rechecked his course on a navigation chart, working with dividers. Deirdre read the message from the carrier pigeon, *"Dreadnought's* making seven knots," she informed the German. The turbine-powered *Dreadnought* was capable of much higher speeds—up to twenty-one knots, but while in the confined waters of the firth, until she reached the open sea, her speed would remain more modest.

He grabbed a notepad and started calculating. "She'll pass us in …"

"Ten to fifteen minutes, depending on the current."

Von Traeger dropped the pad and pencil to the table in annoyance. "Perhaps you would care to command the U-boat, as well!"

She ignored that. "You had better cast off. Have you confirmed your final arrangements?"

Von Traeger resented her questioning him. He prided himself on efficiency. That was, after all, what Prussians were known for. He huffed and allowed, "*Ja.* After the attack, I will make for the sea and rendezvous with my yacht. Once on board, I will scuttle the U-boat, destroying all evidence. Neither Germany nor England will be the wiser."

She nodded in approval. He clicked his heels, *"Möge der Tag bringen uns Glück!"*

"Do as you were instructed and luck will not be a concern. You are squandering time, Baron." She made a small gesture, motioning him toward the U-boat.

Having been thus dismissed, Von Traeger marched to the sub and battened down the hatch. Men cast off mooring lines and jumped to the shore. The sub's internal combustion engine sputtered to life, water bubbled white around her stern, and she began to move down the lagoon toward the cave entrance and the firth beyond.

Deirdre caressed her crescent-moon pendant, watching in satisfaction. The pieces were all falling into place, as she knew they would.

Blake was undoing Tasha's bonds so that she could feed herself from the large wooden bowl of porridge steaming on the nearby stout table.

"Did you pass a good night, ma'am?" asked Blake. He was a simple man at heart who had nothing against Tasha; she was simply on the wrong side. He unfettered one of her arms. "Porridge, ma'am. Have to keep your strength up, you know."

"Very true, and I am sorry for this," she said, and then spun around with her free hand grasping the back of Blake's head. With perfect accuracy, Mother slammed his face into the sturdy bowl of porridge. Focusing all of her considerable strength into the one arm and bracing herself, Tasha forced him under.

Tasha had no personal dislike of Blake. He was merely an obstacle to be overcome. She was fighting to stop a slaughter that would ravage Europe, but she was also a mother protecting her child. She needed freedom of action, and to achieve that, Blake had to die. All of Mother's impressive powers were focused on that goal and Blake was doomed. Tasha strained—her mouth a straight determined line. Without oxygen, Blake weakened and his struggles waned. When they ceased, Mother lifted his face from the bowl. A mass of glistening red pulp lay where his nose used to be. She let the body slide to the floor, freed her other arm, and methodically rifled Blake's pockets. She took his revolver, finding—to her surprise—it was her own Webley Bulldog. Ian must have given it to Blake after she had been disarmed. Then she left the now lifeless chamber.

As Tasha entered the connecting passageway, she was spotted by one of Deirdre's armed men. He was most likely a poacher, for he silently stalked her, shikari-like, as she exited the prison chamber, keeping close to the wall.

She halted, sensing him, and turned, but he ducked behind a projection of rock. Mother hurried on, rounding a sharp corner. He crept up cautiously, and lingered on his side of the corner, listening for any sign of her. The game was cat-and-mouse, but now he wasn't certain which was which. He cocked his revolver, leapt round the corner and landed like a cat, gun ready. He was good, but what he saw surprised him, for he saw nothing. The tunnel was empty. There was no hint of Mother, nor was there any place for her to hide that he could see. He nervously trod into the tunnel, his head oscillating from side-to-side.

If the cult member had been alert to the cavern roof, he would have seen her above him, clinging to irregularities in the rock like some incredible insect. She soundlessly dropped down behind him, leaned close to his ear and whispered: "Boo."

Startled, he jumped, but before his feet touched down, her fist smashed into his jaw, sending him sprawling.... The expression, even then, was down for the count.

The tunnel emptied onto a wide ledge in the main chamber that ran uphill and terminated over the open maw of the sea entrance. There were crates and equipment all about Tasha, as well as sticks of cordite connected by fuse wire. A workman loitered at the far end. Tasha exited the passage and ducked behind some crates. One of the crates was open, and she spotted sticks of dynamite. She stashed a couple of sticks in her belt. One never knew when a large explosion might be convenient.

Back in the passage, three more armed guards found their unconscious compatriot on the tunnel floor. No amount of persuasion would rouse him. They drew their revolvers and rushed down the tunnel.

The little U-boat had nearly reached the mouth the cave, and open water lay beyond. Above it, on the ledge, a workman lit his pipe, watching the sub while leaning against a large crate. Tasha, suddenly behind him, wrapped her arms around his neck and dragged him under cover. While keeping her hand over his mouth to prevent him from alerting the others, she snapped the worker's neck, searched his pockets, and found the box of wooden Vesta matches he used to light his pipe.

Bullets started flying around her. The guards had spotted Mother and were racing toward her while shooting. Tasha used the workman's body as a shield, then tossed the dead cultist aside and bolted to the top of the ledge.

Deirdre, alerted by the firing, spotted Tasha across the lagoon, rushing to the edge of the ledge as the guards closed in. She calculated all of Tasha's options and her counter-measures. Then Deirdre saw Tasha rush to a case of cordite and target it with her Webley. The guard's bullets were already striking near the explosives. Deirdre yelled at her followers. "Stop firing! You'll blow us to atoms!" Her men halted at their priestess's command.

Tasha yelled to Deirdre, "Stop that U-boat or I'll fire!"

Deirdre had already played this scenario in her mind. "It's a poor bluff, Lady Dorrington. You might kill Laura." Then she ordered her men, "Take her!"

Tasha had not really expected Deirdre to believe that she would fire, but it was a move she had to play. The gamble bought a little time, and she used it to back further away from the men and toward the ledge. Deirdre's acolytes closed in. Below her, the sub was just passing under the cave mouth.

Tasha pivoted, shoved the gun into her belt and dove into the lagoon. She swam to the sub and grasped a diving fin. Bullets splashed and whizzed all around. Tasha hung on as the U-boat cleared the cave. She felt cleansed by the cold water, and the open sky above was a liberating contrast to the oppressive confinement of the death-cult's caverns.

Deirdre watched in helpless fury. Tasha had used the one strategy that might be effective, though the odds were heavily against her.

CHAPTER THIRTY-NINE

The U-Boat & *H.M.S. Dreadnought* & The Caverns

The interior of the little boat was incredibly cramped and very noisy. The din of the internal combustion engine reverberated loudly in the tight space. It was a wise choice to employ the midgets, again wearing their miniature German sailor uniforms, as crew members. For between them, the diesel engines, the electric motors, the batteries, the periscope, the two eighteen-inch torpedoes, and myriad valves, pipes, wheels and controls, Von Traeger had little room for his stocky frame to move. The Prussian heard a thumping from the deck above him.

"Himmel. Vas ist das?" he said as he stepped to the hatch ladder.

On deck, Tasha, her clothes soaked and clinging to her, shivered from the cold water and wind as she set the dynamite at the base of the conning tower. Behind her, Von Traeger opened the hatch. He spotted her hopelessly trying to ignite one of the wet matches. He pulled out a seaman's knife and drew back to toss it, but in doing so, struck the lid of the hatch. Tasha, hearing the clang, fired at him. He ducked back into the sub, slamming the hatch behind him. Tasha heard the hatch being secured from the inside. A few seconds later, atop the conning tower, the periscope started to rotate.

Down below, Von Traeger realised that Tasha would be unable to light the fuse. He dismissed the thought of her standing on the deck, firing into the dynamite and committing suicide, and returned to his mission. He spotted the *Dreadnought* in the periscope. Etched on the glass were range-finder markings. The *Dreadnought* sailed into the crosshairs. He would shortly have the range.

Sebastian, on the wing of the *Dreadnought's* bridge, spotted the sub.

A rating, at a pair of binoculars mounted on a swivel stand, checked the coordinates etched into a metal faceplate at the top of the stand and shouted, "Sir! Ship bearing green one-five-oh!"

"It's a bloody U-boat!" yelled Sebastian in mock surprise as he dashed into the wheelhouse.

Summerlee, also on the bridge, gaped at him in confusion, "In British waters?"

Summerlee, Ramsgate, Mycroft, and Bernard rushed to the ports, training binoculars, or simply looking to the coordinates.

"Green one-five-oh?" asked a perplexed Bernard.

Sebastian wondered how this man ever survived in the navy. "Green is starboard—to the right," he offered.

Mycroft took over Sebastian's binoculars. "It's German, all right."

Summerlee snatched up a phone. "Why didn't the lookouts spot this?"

The lookouts in the spotting top were lost in thick, black, oily smoke from the stack. The two ratings were covered in black soot. One of them yelled into the phone, "What submarine, sir?"

Summerlee hung up the phone. "They're having problems up there."

Mycroft contemplated the sub and mused, "Why are they here? And on the surface—plain as day!"

Sebastian took advantage. "Looks like the Huns want us to know they mean business."

"Business?" asked Ramsgate. "We're not at war!"

"Not yet," said Mycroft thoughtfully.

The phone buzzed and a sailor, snatching the receiver from its cradle on the bulkhead, answered, listened, and responded, "Yes, sir," then held the receiver to the Captain. Summerlee grabbed the phone. "Captain." He listened, then covered the phone and motioned to Mycroft. "Mr. Holmes … It's their Lordships. What should I tell them?"

"Tell them you'll call back," said Mycroft agreeably.

It was the best advice anyone had ever given Summerlee. Sebastian was quite satisfied at the U-boat's effect. All was as Deirdre had predicted and planned; vengeance for an ancient treachery was coming to pass before his eyes. Things couldn't be going better.

Tasha, masked from the *Dreadnought's* view by the sub's conning tower, realised that the dynamite was useless and was trying another strategy. If she couldn't kill this metal beast, perhaps she could blind it. She climbed atop the conning tower and, using the butt of her gun, smashed the glass on the periscope.

Von Traeger, acting on instinct, jerked his head away from the eyepiece. "She's smashed the shield!" He sternly peered at his diminutive crew. "Go topside and get her!"

The little sailors exchanged perturbed looks, then, in unison, glanced to Von Traeger and shook their heads "no." He was incredulous. "But that was an order! Everyone obeys orders!"

"You get her, guv'ner!" exclaimed one of the midgets. "She's got a bloody gun up there!"

It was a minor midget mutiny.

"No matter—if I must, I can calculate the range without final adjustment! Open outer doors," said Von Traeger as he removed a stop-watch from his pocket and counted the seconds. One of the midgets moved to the firing lever.

Von Traeger shouted, *"Torpedieren entfernt!"* as he signaled by snapping down his arm. The midget smashed down the lever and the ship vibrated as the torpedo was launched with a hiss of compressed air.

Tasha, her heart in her mouth, saw the torpedo streak toward the battleship. The ship vibrated and a second missile fired.

Summerlee lowered his binoculars and yelled to the Quartermaster, "Hard a-port! Full speed!"

The helmsman repeated the order for clarity and spun the wheel as the telegraph rang down to the engine room for full speed. The ship heeled over. Bernard moaned and slumped over the rail, very, very sick and terrified.

Mycroft was still at the binoculars. "Half the government saw that U-boat fire at us!"

A calm Sebastian watched, silently pleased. He thought he had spotted someone atop the U-boat conning tower, but in the excitement of the oncoming torpedo, that was a detail ignored by all.

The battleship, responding to her innovative double rudders, with white water bubbling and churning in its wake, heeled over as the torpedoes sped toward the rapidly swinging stern.

Mycroft, Ramsgate, Bernard, Sebastian, Summerlee, the Exec, the crew … everyone braced themselves for the impact.

Von Traeger watched the seconds tick away on his stopwatch. He could imagine Deirdre, in the cavern, watching through a telescope, perhaps clutching her crescent-moon pendant in anticipation.

Tasha watched, trying to calculate the angle of attack and the closing speed of the torpedoes against the growing speed of the battleship. The press reports stated that the new twin rudder system would add to the ship's manoeuverability, and her turbines to her speed. These systems would be getting a test, and far earlier than the men who built them ever imagined. The turbines were significantly more responsive than the earlier reciprocating engines that Von Traeger was used to. They gave the battleship just the speed advantage she needed.

The torpedoes only barely missed the stern.

Tasha allowed herself a sigh of relief.

Von Traeger's attention was riveted to his stopwatch. The seconds ticked by and there was no explosion. The truth dawned. "Hmmm. We missed." He could now imagine a fuming Deirdre calling him a Prussian imbecile! But then he recalled that Deidre had already taken this contingency into account. She realised that the simple act of firing on the *Dreadnought* would be enough to precipitate a crisis. The lack of casualties or major damage, or even the sinking of the *Dreadnought*, were mere details. Even a failed attack was, after all, an act of war.

As Sebastian concealed his disappointment, Summerlee growled to his Executive Officer, "Fire on that ship!"

"Aye, aye, sir!" came the crisp reply as the Exec lifted the phone and called fire control.

Ramsgate, who had been reading about the *Dreadnought* as part of his investigation of the naval murders, asked Bernard, "Have the guns been calibrated yet?"

Bernard, incapable of speech, was having trouble recalling the answer. He gagged, put his hand to his mouth and rushed again to the rails.

The core of the *Dreadnought* was her five twin twelve-inch gun-turrets. In an era when battleships carried only four big guns, she carried ten.

Inside the turrets was a clockwork of precision movement: men and machine were fused into one efficient mechanism. Twelve-inch shells, weighing eight hundred and fifty pounds apiece, came up hoists from the ready ammunition magazine below the turret. Men slid them into the guns, and rammers shoved them further up the breech. This was followed by silken containers of cordite, two to each gun, which were slipped up and rammed in. The loading ramps fell away, the huge breeches slammed shut, and the guns elevated.

"Right gun ready!" "Left gun ready!" reported the gunners.

Bernard staggered back from the rail, wiping his chin with a handkerchief. In a hoarse voice, he related to Ramsgate that calibrating the range-finders with the guns was scheduled for the firing range the next day. At that second, the "gun ready" lights flashed on the fire-control table.

"If the range-finders and guns haven't been calibrated, those shells could go anywhere!" said Ramsgate in alarm. He turned to Summerlee, but was too late. The captain yelled, "Fire!"

The Exec repeated into the phone, "Fire!"

At that second, eight of the *Dreadnought's* ten twelve-inch guns—all that could fire on any given side of the ship—erupted, spitting black smoke and flame as the shells were hurled skyward. The crash from those enormous pieces of artillery was deafening, and the entire ship staggered.

One shell exploded near the sheep pen on McGloury's croft.

On High Street, the old doctor was entering the Millport Historical Society when a shell exploded several blocks away behind him, creating a large crater in the cobblestones. As his back was turned, he failed to notice.

On another part of the island, an old man carried a newspaper and hurried toward an outhouse. A shrill whine sped overhead and suddenly the outhouse exploded. The old man shrugged and walked back the way he came.

Summerlee implacably lowered his binoculars. "Uh ... you

may cease fire, Number One."

"Aye. Aye, sir!" came the ever crisp reply.

Summerlee folded his hands behind his back and stood the perfect picture of dignity. Britannia ruled the waves.

One shell, through sheer happenstance, was more accurate and exploded near the sub, sending up a great tower of white water that drenched the ship. Tasha, matches and all, huddled in the conning tower as spray and shell splinters slammed into the sub.

Inside, the little ship heaved at the concussion. The crew tumbled into a pile with Von Traeger on top and the midgets on the bottom. Jets of water spurted from several leaks, drenching them.

Von Traeger was able to stop some of the leaks by using cut-off valves, but the water kept shooting in near the bow. He realised that a fragment from the near miss must have breached the little hull, far more fragile than the stouter hulls of the full-sized submarines. He would never make the rendezvous with his yacht in the open sea, and there was no spot in the firth he could beach the U-boat without risking capture. Nearby was Millport Island, but sheer cliffs were ahead of him and he would sink before reaching any location he could beach the sub. He ordered them back to base. Von Traeger was a man who could make instant decisions, but seemed to have trouble planning more than ten minutes ahead.

The little U-boat manoeuvered back toward the cave as Deirdre, observing the lagoon entrance, drew away from her telescope in disbelief. The incredible fool was coming back and leading the British Navy right to her. She was prepared even for that. Tom, McGloury's hired hand, was working nearby, cleaning away breakfast. She snapped her fingers. He ceased his labours and with a slight bow, turned toward her. "You know what to do.

Lay charges at the ruin entrance and connect them to the cordite in this chamber, then evacuate the cave. They'll send a landing party from the *Dreadnought*. Alert the marksmen on the platform to deal with them."

"They'll stop 'em, Priestess."

Deirdre smiled slightly at his confidence. "If they don't, when we seal the cavern, it will be their tomb. The first of many."

Tom nodded, but something troubled him. "Priestess, these caverns have been our shrine and refuge since the beginning ..."

"... and if we must sadly bid them farewell, take comfort in knowing our enemies are trapped within for eternity, and that our faith is stronger than mere stone."

Tom brightened at that. "Forgive me my doubts, Priestess."

Deirdre nodded and motioned him away. He hurried off to do her bidding. Armed men would soon be taking up their pre-assigned positions. A graduate of Sandhurst, the Royal Military Academy, could not have planned a more efficient defence.

The sub approached the cave entrance, difficult to spot amid the craggy cliffs and stones that rose from the water, masking a direct view of the cavern. Tasha tossed aside the useless matches, took the dynamite, which was only damp, and with all her formidable strength, flung it to the rocks near the cave entrance. She aimed her Webley (almost useless at long range) and fired at the explosives. She needed to take two shots, but they detonated.

On the *Dreadnought's* bridge, the explosion, as Mother intended, caught everyone's attention.

"What the devil was that?" demanded Captain Summerlee.

Sebastian scowled; everything was going to pieces. While he could not see Mother, he knew that she must be responsible. Rage erupted within him. He had watched helplessly as Tasha obsessed his beloved Priestess; had desperately tried to warn Deirdre of the danger Mother represented. Sebastian's counsel went unheeded, and in his failure he now witnessed the ruination of Deirdre's ambitious yet careful planning. Gone was the glorious future she had promised, and that he and his fellow believers had laboured with such devotion to make manifest. But he kept the ferocity of his wrath hidden, for he might yet have a way to influence events. Beside him Ramsgate yelled, "It's hard to spot, but there's a cave in that cliff!"

Mycroft, his voice as dispassionate as ever, noted, "Yes. The U-boat's headed right for it. We may have a solution to this problem after all. Captain, send an armed landing party into that cave."

Summerlee wasn't used to taking orders from civilians, but he knew better than debating Mycroft Holmes, so he nodded in agreement.

Sebastian stepped toward him. "Permission to go with them, sir! I grew up in this area and may be able to help!"

"Very well."

Sebastian saluted and left as the rest returned to their binoculars.

As the sub slid into the cavern, Tasha, holstering the Webley in her belt, dove from the conning tower and swam to the nearby cliff-side. The deck hatch slowly opened, and Von Trigger reconnoitered, spotting Tasha in the water. With the periscope out of commission he conned the boat from above, shouting directions to the midget helmsman below, guiding the sub into the passage. "Two degrees to port!" and the bow of the sub—low in the water from the leak and with her forward decks awash—swung in alignment with the tunnel opening.

CHAPTER FORTY

The Caverns

Men rushed about in disciplined activity, stringing new cable, mooring the sub, and making preparations to evacuate. Marksmen, with armbands reading "Millport Skeet Society," found cover on the platform, awaiting the landing party. Two men ripped a canvas cover from a Maxim machine-gun and trained it on the lagoon.

MAXIM
MACHINE-GUN

Below them, Deirdre, aware of the imminent battle, had decided how the altered circumstances would affect me. She stopped McGloury and gave him orders, "Take Laura to the sacrificial chamber and wait for me. If Ian hasn't fallen, cut the rope. If you don't hear from me in ten minutes, kill the child."

McGloury was not enthusiastic. "The child ... Please—this isnae a task for me, Priestess."

"There is a penalty for disobedience," she said quietly. Under her inflexible expectation of servility, he could only nod.

Ian was desperately trying to save himself as the flame burned through the rope that circled his waist. His life depended on the durability of a few strands of hemp. With his hands tied behind his back, Ian—his time on the range leaving him no stranger to the use of cordage—worked his fingers to loosen the knots. He gave a fleeting glance to the flame as another strand separated; there was little of the fibre left. At last the knots loosened and Ian worked his hands free. He reached for the line from the pulley above him and climbed.

The rope snapped, but Ian was able to grasp the pulley attached to the ceiling. He saw the empty darkness below his feet where the rope, still tied to his waist, now swayed. Ian shifted his weight and swung back and forth like a pendulum. The metal of the pulley sliced into his hand. When he could bear no more pain, he let go and plummeted.

Ian's swing carried him just far enough to grasp the ledge of the pit. The jagged edge bit deeper into his bleeding hands, but Ian hung on, ignoring the pain. The ancient stone under his right hand crumbled in his grip. He caught himself with his left hand, dangling with only the strength of one arm between him and the blackness below. But the stone under his left hand held him solidly. Using both arms, Ian pulled himself up, listening to the pounding of his own heart as the blood rushed in his ears. He paused, kneeling on the edge of the pit, breathing hard, collecting his thoughts. Then he untied the rope. In an instinct honed by years in the saddle, he coiled the remains of the rope, slung it over his shoulder and rushed out of the chamber.

Deirdre spotted, past the cavern opening, the distant motor-launch from the *Dreadnought* speeding toward them. She could see the scarlet tunics of the Royal Marines clumped together with the armed ratings that formed the small landing party.

Tasha climbed out of the firth onto a narrow ridge that widened as it led away from the water and into the huge chamber. She heard voices from around the corner and stopped, flattening herself against the craggy stone side of the cavern. Some men were attaching new cable to crates of cordite.

"That's the job. Put the plunger in the crypt, then Deirdre said to get topside," said one.

"Aye! That's the truth!" said the other. "Once our priestess touches this off, the old place will ..." He gestured, imitating the expanding violence of an explosion.

That was it then, thought Mother; she knew it was a race against time with my life at stake. She listened to the men leave, then silently followed.

I don't really remember any of this; Deirdre's drugs clouded my mind to such an extent that I was a little automaton. But as I understand what happened, McGloury led me into the sacrificial chamber and placed me in front of the pit. McGloury noted the broken rope, and assuming Ian's fate, eyed the pit, not really expecting to see any sign of him in the blackness. He had every intention of carrying out his priestess's instructions—blind devotion and raw fear would allow no less—and though Deirdre had not desired mercy, her latest command would spare me the horrible fate of becoming her.

To the two dozen officers, ratings, and Royal Marines in the motor-launch sailing through the lagoon to the pier, the immense chamber appeared empty. But atop the platform, under the concealment of stacks of boxes and rocky outcroppings—wherever nature or human efforts provided cover—Deirdre's marksmen were ready. Their rifles and the Maxim machine-gun were trained on the dock, waiting for the marines to disembark. They had been careful to shield the cordite (which Deirdre would explode with a plunger) behind rocks and equipment. A lucky shot or ricochet could still turn the lagoon into an inferno, but that was a calculated risk that these deluded men were willing to take to honour their beliefs.

The head marksman whispered to his men, "By McGuffin's great axe! Sebastian's with them! Be careful, lads."

In the crypt chamber, the hollow eye-sockets of countless skeletons witnessed Deirdre nimbly attaching the wire to the twin poles of the detonator. Behind her, men were making their escape as they filed out of the crypt and climbed up the shaft. Some gave their priestess a confident grin, others were sad, but all showed deference. Then came the sound of gunfire. Her followers instinctively swung their attention in the direction of the main chamber. The muffled clamour of battle intensified. Deirdre merely finished her work on the plunger.

The Royal Marines and the rest of the landing party jumped off the launch and moved cautiously into the great chamber. They did not speak, though their sergeant gave his men silent hand signals, ordering them to spread out; clumped together they were too inviting a target.

As the British contingent separated, Deirdre's men erupted into action. Rifles cracked and the Maxim rattled, and the Marines and ratings below began to fall, or to find what cover they could on the pier and among their dead comrades who littered the pilings. Sebastian crouched behind a crate as a marine jumped next to him and returned fire. The other marines and the rifle-armed ratings also were shooting.

Above them, on the platform, one of Deirdre's men was hit and toppled to the chamber floor far below, landing with a thud heard amid the din of battle.

Sebastian kept his head down, awaiting any opportunity to aid his cause, find Deirdre, or kill Mother.

All but one of the cult members had fled up the shaft that led to the ruins and escape. As the last man, a large rustic in a sheepskin vest, started up, he noted that Deirdre wasn't following. "I heard Sebastian was with the landing party," he told her. "I'm sure our men'll take care not to hit him."

She nodded and motioned for him to hurry up the shaft. He took a step, but paused again and with genuine regret in his eyes, "Sorry there was a wee change in your wonderful plans, Priestess. We're still with you."

"An inconvenience, nothing more. Our destiny and revenge still await us." She again gestured for him to climb away. The big man gave a curt nod and vanished upward.

A few feet away, on the other side of the door, a devotee wearing a sidearm was still guarding any approach to the crypt chamber. Deirdre had given him permission to leave, but he and a few others in various parts of the caverns stayed anyway, determined to guard her to the last. Further down the tunnel, Tasha stepped out of the shadows, raised her Webley and fired. The guard dropped lifeless to the ground. Mother raced to the door, but the wounded man sprung back to life, lunging for her leg and taking her down. As she fell, he backhanded her with his own revolver. Mother reeled, but put her gun to his head and fired. She pushed his heavy, lifeless body away and leaned, gasping against the wall. Without warning, the wooden shaft of a harpoon smashed the gun from her hand. Tom was there, clutching the weapon, turning the Lili-iron with its sharp metal barb toward her.

"Welcome back, ma'am." He grinned and jabbed the metal barb toward her stomach. Tasha bent away as he swung it, but the harpoon cut a painful slash in her left arm. Mother grabbed the wound and felt her warm, wet blood trickling down her hand. Tom moved in for the kill.

As he jabbed, she grabbed the long wooden shaft and swung him into the wall. He was stronger than she thought, for he kept hold of the harpoon and struck Mother in the jaw with its wooden end. Mother staggered, but forced herself to recover. She lunged toward him and kicked the harpoon from his grasp. It fell to the ground. They both dove for the spear. Mother was quicker. She got it, rolled along the ground, raised the weapon, and impaled Tom in mid-leap. The harpoon ran him through, protruding from his back. He clutched it and fell against a crate, pinned like an insect on a collector's card.

Down the tunnel, another man ran toward Tasha, his knife poised to throw. She retrieved her gun, fired, and hit him just as he threw his blade. Mother somersaulted away, and without stopping, smashed feet-first into the crypt door.

The ancient wood gave way. Tasha landed on her feet. Deirdre spun to her, caught off guard by Tasha's sudden appearance. They both froze.

"Where is my daughter?" Tasha asked grimly.

"Here—forever!" Deidre replied with a glimmer of glee on her face. She reached for the plunger as Tasha raised her gun and fired. But the shot didn't stop Deirdre from depressing the plunger. The mad priestess laughed in triumph. "You missed."

Tasha's grim face slowly softened into a humourless smile. All was still. There was no explosion.

Deirdre's triumphant smirk faded as she gave a quick glance down at the plunger. Mother had shot away the wire connecting the detonator to the cordite. Deirdre looked up, and their eyes locked.

"Laura," said Tasha in a harsh whisper.

The priestess remained silent and motionless.

Mother hurled her revolver to the floor, and with an insane, unwavering gaze, advanced on Deirdre.

Deirdre held her ground; her arm slipped from the detonator handle to her side, releasing a long needle from her sleeve into her hand. "This'll put a smile on your face," she hissed.

Mother stopped.

Tier upon tier of ancient skeletons surrounded the two women. In this chamber of death, they stood motionless, like coiled serpents. Then Mother screamed like an enraged animal and sprung upon Deirdre, smashing her to the ground. The poisoned needle clattered out of her hand. Deirdre struggled, visibly afraid; she was no match for the fury she had unleashed in Tasha.

Mother lost all control, attacking with berserker rage. I am glad I did not see it. At that moment she wasn't thinking of me, or of anything. Her mind, usually in such command, was overwhelmed by the very emotions it spent such energy repressing. She slammed Deirdre into the cave wall, smashed her head to the ground and pounded on her in a frenzy long after Deirdre had lost consciousness.

Then Tasha stopped. Perhaps it was the warmth of the blood on her hands, but some deep sense forced her to cease, knowing that anything further would kill Deirdre, and as much as part of her wanted that, another, more enlightened part, did not. Mother collapsed to the ground, clutching her injured arm, laughing and weeping at the same time. The rage drained away and rationality took control. She heard my name escape from her lips and forced herself once more into action. Trailing blood, Tasha left the chamber.

McGloury heard the muffled sounds of the battle and eyed me as I stood like a statue where he had placed me on the edge of the pit. The time had come for him to act.

The cult marksmen pinned down the landing party below them with murderous fire from the machine gun. Sebastian wisely kept under cover as the marine next to him returned fire. The crack of his lone Lee-Enfield was answered by a fusillade from the Maxim.

"We can 'ardly 'it 'em from down 'ere, sir!" the marine complained to Sebastian. As he ducked down, the top of the wooden crate he was using for cover was splintered by machine gun rounds. Then the whirr of the Maxim suddenly stilled.

On the platform, the ammunition belt feeding continuous death from the Maxim ran out and the loader reached into the ammunition box for another. As he did, the box suddenly jerked away from him. He spotted a hook tied to a rope pulling the crate, and before he could utter a word, there was another jerk and the box vanished around a corner. The loader signaled to a marksman and, his rifle at the ready, the rifleman entered the tunnel to investigate.

The marine near Sebastian used the sudden cessation of machine-gun fire to dart deeper into the chamber. He was instantly hit by rifle fire and staggered back atop Sebastian. The commander looked down in disgust as his once immaculate uniform was smeared in blood.

A marksman on the platform lit a stick of dynamite, taken from a box well under cover from the firing. He tossed the makeshift grenade into a cluster of marines who were using a small winch and crane as cover. The explosive detonated in fire and smoke, collapsing the crane and killing most of the marines and sailors.

Mother raced into the small chamber that once held McGloury's collie. There was no sign of me. She had not found anyone in the near-deserted tunnels who could give her any information. Mother was reduced to searching for me, chamber by chamber. Von Traeger stepped out of the shadows, his rapier ready. Tasha faced him and demanded, "Where's Laura?"

He tried to slice her with his blade, but she narrowly avoided his skillful attack.

"You have made a fool of me!" he snarled, but as he swept at her again and again, she dodged him. Tasha spotted his spare rapier on the other side of the chamber, resting against the wall. He saw where she was looking, stepped back, raised his sword in salute and bowed. Mother, ever on guard, picked up the blade. Von Traeger gave her a nasty grin. "*Fräulein*, I am going to enjoy this."

"Dinnae gut your fish till ye get them!" chided Tasha, imitating the local accent.

He growled and lunged, but to his surprise, she parried, and the duel of Von Traeger's life commenced. With cold fury, Mother backed him out of the chamber. She was a grim fighting machine that relentlessly pressed on and on. Von Traeger hid behind a crate and Tasha's blade became stuck as she swung. He used his one advantage, slicing her already injured left arm. That lapse enraged Mother. She was as furious at herself as she was at this arrogant imbecile, and she pressed on with even greater savagery.

As she forced him into retreat, he gasped in amazement, "Impossible ... women cannot fight!"

"There's only one reason you are still alive." She smashed the sword from his hand and snapped her blade between his eyes. He froze. "Now," she said with finality. "Where's Laura?"

In the tunnel, the marksman thought he spotted the Maxim ammunition box ahead of him. Suddenly, he was ensnared in a lariat; Ian decked him with a solid right hook, then rubbed his sore hand. With a sense of purpose, Ian retrieved the rifle and dashed back down the tunnel toward the platform that overlooked the lagoon, where the cultists poured down fire on the Marines and ratings.

As more dynamite exploded, the marines and sailors realised their battle was hopeless and retreated back toward the launch. The cult marksman on the platform ignited the fuse on another stick of dynamite. This had been his own idea, and he was delighted his strategy was working so effectively. He picked his target, a sergeant and two privates racing from the cover of some crates toward the motor-launch. He reached back to toss when a gunshot—ignored among all the other gunshots—cracked. That sound was the last he would ever hear. The bullet went through his brain, and he fell, the explosive pinned beneath him.

Ian, at the tunnel entrance, emptied the rifle into the other marksmen and then ducked back into the shaft as the survivors, now aware of an attack from behind, spun and opened fire on him.

One of the cultists rolled over the body pinning the still burning dynamite. His act was brave—but too late. As he was about to toss the explosive to the Marines below, it ignited in his hand. By some miracle, the explosion did not blow up the nearby cordite, but the Maxim, the marksmen upon the platform, the battle, all vanished in that fateful detonation.

The marines halted their retreat, and with the armed ratings, rallied and swarmed into the chamber. With the cult marksmen's advantage of cover and firepower gone, the few survivors were efficiently routed by the better-trained Marines.

Sebastian fell behind the skirmish, and slipped away into one of the tunnels.

McGloury heard the fighting die away and realised that the game was up. Even so, his devotion to Deirdre was absolute, and he was determined to follow her command. He placed his hands on my waist and lifted me over the pit. I was like a statue and not aware of what was being done to me. But I now know that as he was about to drop me, the blade of a sword thrust through his chest.

Mother had raced into the sacrificial chamber and was there behind us. She grasped me with her injured arm as McGloury toppled into the abyss. The cultist disappeared into the darkness. I can vaguely recall his screams as he plummeted out of sight. I think I can also recall Mother's agony as she pulled me to safety with her injured arm. I did not react, even when Mother embraced me. Had I been in my senses, the sight of my usually composed Mother weeping and thanking God would have been a remarkable sight to me. But that was not what I saw. My distorted mind envisioned the monster again, ripping away my flesh, crushing me until blood was pouring out of my body. Then I screamed! The horror my mindless shriek brought to Mother was as terrible as anything I was imagining. My vision cleared—the monster abruptly vanished—I saw my broken mother with horrible clarity. That piercing sight—paired with the guilt, terror, and anger brought on by the indelible and ghastly image of Mother evoked by Deirdre's potions—would echo in our lives for years to come.

Deirdre, in the crypt chamber, was still on the floor, nearly insensible from the battering Mother had given her. Her fingers stirred, moving through a puddle of her own blood. My scream echoed and distorted in the chamber. Somehow, even through her agony, she managed the ghost of a smile in the knowledge that as injured as she was, the internal wounds she had inflicted on Mother and me would endure far longer.

CHAPTER FORTY-ONE

The Caverns

Ramsgate was angry. "You mean to suppress this, don't you?"

He was speaking to Mycroft Holmes as, along with Captain Summerlee, they walked through the main chamber. All around them, the cave was a beehive of activity. As naval officers examined the partially sunken sub, marines—rifles ready—cautiously searched all the chambers.

Mycroft thumbed through a sheaf of captured documents. "Hmmm?" he asked absent-mindedly.

Ramsgate knew that Mycroft had heard every word, but repeated himself just the same. "I said you intend to suppress this!"

"Of course," Mycroft replied affably. "You can't publicly announce that two of the largest limited companies in the United Kingdom and ..." He perused one paper in particular, "... the third largest concern in Germany, worked amicably with a group of demon worshippers to start a major war. Not good for public confidence."

Ramsgate threw up his hands in futility.

"What would you do, Commissioner?" Mycroft said to Ramsgate with some sympathy, as he handed several pages to Summerlee while gleaning information from the few papers remaining in his hands. "Charge in and arrest the board of directors? Four of them are members of Parliament. Two of them are members of my party. One is a member of my club. We need them. It's that simple."

"Above the law, are they? Still, I'd like to see something done," said Ramsgate in asperity.

"Something will be done. We'll let them know that we know. And with luck, no one else ever will." He stopped walking and turned to face Ramsgate. "I'm concerned about Lady Dorrington's discretion."

Ramsgate instantly sprang to Mother's defence. "I have complete confidence ..."

"She's a woman, Ramsgate. They have their own inscrutable sense of responsibility." Mycroft continued walking, eying the *Dreadnought* papers taken from the murdered commander in St. James Park, "And while we are on the subject ... a very intriguing plan. What an incandescent intelligence this Deirdre has. Malevolent, yet darkly magnificent."

Summerlee shook his head as he read the captured pages in disbelief. "Remarkable. But do you really think a lone woman could have conceived all this?"

Ramsgate was long past that kind of narrow-mindedness. Extended exposure to Mother had done that, but he was smart enough to know when to pick his battles, and said nothing. Mycroft simply commented, "You've plainly spent too much time at sea, Captain."

They came to the detonator, now brought up to the main chamber. Mycroft fingered the device, his eyes twinkling. "I think this Deirdre had a remarkably good idea here."

Outside the cavern, the detonator plunger was depressed and an explosion near the cave entrance sent rocks tumbling down from the cliff, sealing the entrance.

Nearby, Mycroft watched several Royal Marines who were manning three more detonator boxes. An officer signaled and the second detonator was set off.

Inside, an explosion rocked the main chamber. A cave-in started, and boulders battered the U-boat, completing the job of the leak and sending the makeshift craft to the bottom of the lagoon.

Up above, Mycroft nodded in satisfaction as the officer signaled for the last detonator. The final explosion would destroy and seal the evidence. No one would know what happened here, for at least as long as it mattered. Only the ruins near McGloury's cottage remained intact.

The dolmens with their tortured faces are there still.

Chapter Forty-two

Glasgow Central Station

The train whistle blew inside the monumental enclosed platform of Central Station. Scaffolding from the recent enlargement clad the side of the ornate building, and the massive new bridge over the River Clyde was completed, but was not yet open to the public. The Caledonian Railway had made every effort to see to the comfort of its passengers. There was even a first-class hotel, which fronted an entire side of the station. That hotel—with its up-to-date plumbing, elegant restaurant, and comfortable beds, as well as the station with its modern steam trains, connected to an efficient transportation system—was only a few scant miles away from Deirdre, with her macabre caverns, demon-worshipping acolytes, and life-stealing potions.

Ramsgate stood on the platform trying to make small talk with Mother, a woman who, even under pleasing circumstances, disdained idle chatter. Tasha stood before the open doorway of a plush private railroad car attached to the *Royal Scot*. Her left arm, in a sling, was causing her pain. She interrupted Ramsgate and asked him to thank Mycroft Holmes for the use of the private car.

"Since there can't be any public recognition, he felt it was the least he could do. He's rather keen on hushing this up."

Tasha was more than aware of that, and agreed with Mycroft, though not for the same reasons. She simply thought that in the end, exposure or suppression would make no difference in the course of world events.

"How's the arm?" asked Ramsgate.

She smiled, "It's nothing."

"And Laura?"

Her smile faded. She had led me, as if I was walking in my sleep, to a bed in the private car. Mycroft had offered a nurse, but Mother refused. Watching over me was her personal responsibility.

Ramsgate changed tack. "Deirdre isn't being let off. It'll be nineteen fifty before she sees daylight again. What a monster."

Tasha's eyes flashed. "A genius!" she said with bitter admiration. "The way she manipulated those armaments manufacturers; revitalized her cult. The sham case she arranged for me, perfect in almost every detail and arranged on very little notice."

Ramsgate was surprised at Mother's admiration. "Let's be thankful she wasn't too good," was all he could manage.

"It hardly matters; the war will come. Soon. And I don't think this world we know will survive it."

"Why didn't you kill her? I would have."

Mother's lack of response provided no insights.

The final whistle blew from the engine.

"There's someone else who wanted to say goodbye," said Ramsgate as he nodded down the platform. Ian was approaching, flanked by two constables. At Ramsgate's signal, the pair let him walk alone toward Mother. Ramsgate nodded toward Ian. "Mr. Holmes took your suggestion to heart, Tasha."

Tasha closed her eyes, sighed, then tenderly kissed Ramsgate on the forehead. "Thank you."

Ian came close and Ramsgate retreated, leaving them alone. Ian looked self-consciously at Tasha, neither of them comfortable. He let out a breath and finally spoke, "They're sendin' me back to Montana. You wouldn't know anything about that—" he gave her a weak grin.

She did not return his attempt at intimacy, "Let's just say I like to pay my debts."

Ian's smile faded and again there was an uncomfortable pause. This time Tasha spoke first, "Stay there, Ian. Build a new life in the clean air of a new world; escape the storm that will soon wither this old one."

He nodded and they faced each other.

"Goodbye, Tasha." He started to say more, but she held up her hand, stopped him and shook her head. He understood, then gazed into her eyes, trying to read them, but they were also silent.

The train behind Tasha started to move. She stepped into the doorway of the railroad car, watching as Ian—the lone figure on the platform, isolated by white steam—receded into the distance.

Tasha could watch no more. She leaned into the car, her face distant and drained as she whispered, "Adios."

CHAPTER FORTY-THREE

The *Royal Scot*

The train sped south, hooking a mailbag off a passing post. Inside the mail compartment, an old-timer was showing the basics to his dandified young assistant. The old-timer didn't think the lad had much of a future in this career. He didn't seem all that interested and hated to get his hands dirty. As the young man slowly started to sort the mail, the older man tried giving him a word of encouragement. "That's it, lad. Three stacks to start ... London ... across the channel ..."

The assistant held up a letter. "This one's got no stamp."

"Aye! But look at the envelope.... Crest of the Earl of Danoon. Anyone he's writing to is good for the postage. If it's quality, we send it on ..."

The young assistant shrugged and dropped the envelope to the London stack.

Tasha sat in the sleeping compartment of Mycroft's luxurious private car, watching me as I lay trance-like on the bed. The car was divided into two sections: a sitting room in front and a sleeping compartment in the rear, connected by a wide door. From behind Mother came a knock at the passageway door, and a porter's voice announced dinner had been brought to her from the kitchen. Mother had arranged to eat in the compartment; she was in no mood to see people and did not want to be away from me.

"Come in." She turned back to me as the door opened, and Sebastian entered in a porter's uniform. We later found he had killed a genuine porter and tossed his body from the train. He set down the tray, uncovered a dish and drew a revolver from the plate.

Mother heard him order her to turn around. Her body tensed, and she slowly turned. "Well, Commander, 'Journeys end in lovers meeting.'"

He motioned for her to enter the sitting room. Her eyes instinctively darted to me and, not wishing to be near me if there was gunfire, she obeyed. Sebastian signaled her toward the exterior door. Outside the window, the countryside was rushing by in a blur of lights and dark shapes in the night.

"Open the door," he ordered.

Mother did so, magnifying the din of the speeding train. "What will you do with Laura?" she asked as she finished opening the door.

He glared coldly. "What did you do with Deirdre? Kill her?"

"She's alive. She wants you!" Tasha took a step toward him. He wasn't stupid and brandished the gun, stopping Mother cold.

"You destroyed her!" the words spat out of him. "Before her we were nothing—now we'll be nothing again!"

"Then perhaps you'd like to destroy me."

"I intend to."

"With that?" Mother dismissively gestured toward the gun. "Where's the satisfaction?"

He shook his head, not having any of it. Mother dropped her inviting smile and nodded toward me.

"I'd like to say goodbye to Laura." There was no hint of pleading in Mother's voice, which would have been pointless. He would either grant her request or he would not.

"Why should I?" he answered.

"A parent would not ask. Perhaps simple compassion is beyond you," explained Mother.

"Don't move." With the gun trained on her, Sebastian cautiously stepped to the doorway of the sleeping compartment. He momentarily fixed on me, motionless on the bed; then his focus reverted back to Mother. The scowl never left his face, but he signaled his consent to Tasha.

Mother stepped to me, all the while covered by Sebastian's revolver, and sat on the bed. She wrapped her arms around me and kissed me gently on the forehead and then, suddenly, hard on the mouth.

The monster was ripping at my face! My eyes flew open, and I screamed until my tortured throat could not produce another sound.

Sebastian was momentarily stunned, only for a second, but that was all Tasha needed. She ploughed into her larger opponent, smashing the gun from his hand.

"That's what your Deirdre did to her!" cried Mother with intensity. "She can't stand to be touched!"

Sebastian, driven by his own demons, fought back. They struggled through the compartment, knocking over the furnishings and nearly tumbling out the open door. It was a close thing. Mother was exhausted and with one bad arm, fighting to the death against the powerful and insanely determined Sebastian.

He pinned Mother to the floor and wrapped his muscular hands around her throat. She couldn't break his grip and felt darkness closing in around her. Then desperately, with her good arm, she smashed the palm of her hand against his chin, stunning him. She threw him off and, using her powerful legs, kicked him out the open door. His neck caught on a passing mail hook and he flew out of the compartment. He hung there, his eyes open, the hook jutting from his neck, his expression grotesquely bewildered.

Mother collapsed across the bed, drained in mind, body, and heart. I sat next to her, now silent, catatonic, and staring at the wall. Mother had again saved our lives, but there was no feeling of safety for me. Part of me had died. My child's sense of love and security had been shattered, and left me only with fear and—though I later understood how unfair these emotions were—a sense of betrayal. The journey back for both of us would be long. Only when I was older and shared the challenges and dangers of our now mutual profession would my bond with Mother at last truly and completely heal.

As the mail car sped past, Sebastian's body was hooked and flung inside.

The prim young man stared aghast at the body. The older man was in the back, sorting letters.

"Sir ... sir ..." gasped the young man.

The old-timer, while sorting, just repeated, "If it's quality ... send it on."

CHAPTER FORTY-FOUR

Lady Natasha Dorrington's Residence, Grosvenor Square

 few days later, at ten in the morning, Mother was still haggard from her ordeal. She entered her house to see Wickett, our butler, rushing down the stairs toward her. His usually passive demeanour was discernibly upset.

"Oh, Madam ... the police, they've taken away Miss Laura."

Tasha's face hardened. Before she could speak, she saw Mycroft Holmes. He stood phlegmatically at the study door, gesturing for her to enter. Tasha did not move, but stood rooted, collecting her powers. She already had a good idea what was going on, and her blood boiled.

"Please," said Mycroft as he motioned into the study.

Mother walked over warily, while saying, offhandedly to Wickett, "Please continue with the packing."

"Yes," agreed Mycroft. "I think that's best."

She stopped before him, furious, resenting his imperious attitude, and most of all, anxious about me. "Where's Laura, Mr. Holmes?"

"She's getting the best help in England."

"The best is in Vienna."

"But not the most discreet."

She entered the study. Inside were three husky constables—insurance on Mycroft's part. She glared fiercely at him.

If Mycroft was aware of Mother's anger, he did not reveal it. "Please understand I am speaking for exceedingly high-placed personages. My own feelings in the matter are of little moment. They suggested we discuss your retirement." He amiably waved toward Tasha's upholstered armchair.

As Mother sat down, she was instantly flanked on either side by the constables.

Mycroft, as if giving a lecture, continued. "Last week our entire intelligence apparatus was outsmarted by one woman, and rescued by another."

Tasha nodded ironically.

"My ... friends ... wouldn't like this known," Mycroft added.

"My lips are sealed," she said flatly.

Mycroft smiled and settled his capacious bulk comfortably in a chair. "Are they?"

"I want Laura." Mother stripped away all but the essential.

He suavely ignored her comment. "The concern is that you could become famous, Lady Dorrington. And, as a woman, a cause célèbre in some misguided circles. Radical circles that would seek to air your accomplishments before, I believe the term they used was 'the mob.' That kind of notoriety is considered dangerous."

"By your friends?"

Mycroft nodded. "There you have it."

Mother held him under her penetrating inspection. Deep beneath his patrician impassivity was something else: Fear. Tasha smiled enigmatically and leaned back in her chair. Her legs extended, her fingers pressed together in the familiar thoughtful pyramid, she closed her eyes. The lady detective in her favourite thinking position.

Mother had violated convention, not because she had anything to prove, but because she was determined to live the life she wanted; to use her gifts in the way she saw fit. But her unrelenting challenges to a culture which sought to crush that spirit—and her own arrogance—had exacted a savage price on her—and on me.

Mother would never again allow her child to be vulnerable. The crucible of Deirdre had mandated changes; her nights at the Inn of Illusion were done, that energy was now dedicated to my well-being, but she would not abandon the passion of her calling.

Mycroft breathed heavily, reminding Mother of his presence.

She did not fear Mr. Holmes or the shadowy authorities for which he spoke. Mother leaned forward, holding Mycroft in her uncompromising gaze, and though the motion was slight, she defiantly shook her head.

Epilogue

Lady Laura Dorrington's Residence, Grosvenor Square

1982

Tasha's chair, repaired and reupholstered in the intervening near eighty years, still remained rooted in its spot in the study. The rest of the room had altered. Gone were the Edwardian pieces and the bric-a-brac, replaced by modern furnishings: a stereo, television, and even that very latest of devices, a computer. Outside the window, near a full-length oil portrait of Tasha, the Bentley carrying Laura and Julian pulled up.

The driver opened the door for Laura, but she sat for moment as she remembered.

"Julian, you've made me call up a lot of ghosts." Her mind was distant and her voice was far away. "But it was useful to reflect back, with the wisdom of now, on the wounds of then."

She stepped out of the car and walked to her house. Julian accompanied her to the door. "Laura. That's a horrid place to stop. What happened ... with her ... with you?"

Laura paused in the doorway as another memory altered her mood. Her eyes suddenly twinkled, "Ah, that's another story."

She entered the house she had known since childhood and softly closed the door.

AFTERWORD

In 1906 the two superpowers of the Edwardian age, Great Britain and Germany, were in the beginnings of an arms race that had parallels in the military rivalry of the Cold War that dominated the latter half of the twentieth century.

Germany, a land power, was building a fleet to challenge the naval supremacy of Britain—a move that a maritime power like Britain could not safely ignore.

Under the energetic direction of First Sea Lord, Admiral John Fisher, Britain answered the German challenge in the form of the *H.M.S. Dreadnought*, one of the most remarkable ships in the history of the world.

Completed in the remarkably short span of a year and a day, the *Dreadnought*, with her new turbine engines (a first), her massive firepower (twice that of any existing ship), and her numerous other innovations made all previous battleships obsolete. If the Kaiser wanted to compete with Britain, then he would have to answer with dreadnoughts of his own.

Germany did just that. The rivalry that followed gripped the attention of the world. The two superpowers invested gigantic sums in the construction of these sea-going monsters. The size of the fleets, the range of the guns and all the deadly statistics were heralded by the press, as the populations of both countries studied the figures and hoped that the sum of these numbers equaled security.

Lady Sherlock is fiction, but the story has a genesis in reality. The facts relating to the *Dreadnought* and the public's reaction to her are history.

The end-result of this arms race is also history—the conflagration was called, at the time, The Great War.

We call it World War One.

ADDENDUM

About the Artwork in *Lady Sherlock*

Inclusion of visuals was inspired by the legacy of the richly illustrated Sherlock Holmes stories as they first appeared in Strand Magazine.

The author personally crafted a majority of the images in this book. Most of the graphics contain elements well over a century old. In many instances the backgrounds were created using bits and pieces from dozens of Victorian photos. These public-domain vintage photographs were combined with recently taken pictures depicting our heroine. All of these elements were composited in Photoshop, sometimes colorized (for the E-book edition), and then given an engraving overlay to complete the period effect.

The cover is based on *A Wet Night on the Embankment* by Paul Martin. Shot around 1895, this photograph is a rare Victorian time-exposure taken at night.

It is hoped that the illustrations will enhance a modern reader's experience, helping them step back into that long-vanished era of swirling London fogs, Hansom Cabs, and the singular adventures of Lady Natasha Dorrington.

ABOUT THE AUTHOR

Lady Sherlock: Circle of the Smiling Dead may be Brooks Wachtel's first novel, but he is no stranger to crafting stories; he is an Emmy Award-winning writer with a long resume in television and film.

Mr. Wachtel spent his youth as a "Navy Brat" traveling the world. While attending Hollywood High School and college he produced several student films. One, a forty-five minute Sherlock Holmes

Photo by Steven L. Sears

spoof was the first film ever shot at Hollywood's famed Magic Castle.

Wachtel co-created, executive produced, and co-wrote many episodes of the hit series *DogFights* for the History Channel. He also wrote and produced many History Channel documentaries, including episodes of *Defending America: National Guard* and *The Coast Guard*. Additionally, he has written *The Great Ships*, *Search and Rescue*, *The Royal Navy*, and *Fly Past*, which won the Cine Golden Eagle Award.

Wachtel also wrote and co-produced an independent documentary feature illustrating the history of his famous alma-mater, *Hollywood High School*. All rights and royalties were donated to Hollywood High to help fill the school's scholarship funds.

His latest documentary project, *Silver Tsunami*, which he co-wrote and co-produced, details the calamity of the massive and aging baby-boomer demographic.

In addition, Wachtel has written more than 100 produced episodes of television fiction—with shows as diverse as Fox's live-action *Young Hercules* (starring Ryan Gosling), to animated hits like PBS's *Liberty's Kids*, *Tutenstein*, *Heavy Gear*, *Spider-Man*, *X-Men*, *Robo-Cop*, and *Beast Machines: Transformers*. For younger viewers, he has penned episodes of the pre-school hits, *Clifford the Big Red Dog* and *Rainbow Fish*. His work on *Tutenstein* received an Emmy Award.

Wachtel serves on the Steering Committee of the Animation Writers Caucus of the Writers Guild, as well as teaching screenwriting at UCLA Extension. He is a performing magician and member of Hollywood's Magic Castle.

IF YOU LIKED ...

If you liked *Lady Sherlock*, you might also enjoy:

Best of Penny Dread
Blood Ties
Clockwork Angels

OTHER WORDFIRE PRESS TITLES

Our list of other WordFire Press authors and titles is always growing. To find out more and to see our selection of titles, visit us at:

wordfirepress.com